Jacob M. Manning

Peace Under Liberty

Oration delivered before the city authorities of Boston, on the Fourth of

July, 1865

Jacob M. Manning

Peace Under Liberty
Oration delivered before the city authorities of Boston, on the Fourth of July, 1865

ISBN/EAN: 9783337224714

Printed in Europe, USA, Canada, Australia, Japan

Cover: Foto ©Andreas Hilbeck / pixelio.de

More available books at **www.hansebooks.com**

Peace under Liberty.

ORATION

DELIVERED BEFORE THE

CITY AUTHORITIES OF BOSTON,

ON THE

FOURTH OF JULY, 1865,

BY

J. M. MANNING.

TOGETHER WITH

AN ACCOUNT OF THE MUNICIPAL CELEBRATION OF THE EIGHTY-NINTH ANNIVERSARY

OF

AMERICAN INDEPENDENCE.

BOSTON:
J. E. FARWELL & COMPANY, PRINTERS,
No. 37 CONGRESS STREET.

1865.

CITY OF BOSTON.

—

In Common Council, July 6, 1865.

ORDERED: That the thanks of the City Council be presented to the Rev. Jacob M. Manning for the highly eloquent and patriotic Oration delivered by him before the Municipal authorities on the celebration of the Declaration of American Independence, July 4, 1865, and that he be requested to furnish a copy for publication.

Sent up for concurrence.

WM. B. FOWLE, *President.*

In Board of Aldermen, July 10, 1865.

Concurred.

G. W. MESSINGER, *Chairman.*

Approved July 11, 1865.

F. W. LINCOLN, JR., *Mayor.*

A true copy. Attest:

S. F. McCLEARY, *City Clerk.*

ORATION.

HERETOFORE on occasion of our National Anniversary the speakers summoned to address you have sometimes pressed on your hearing ideas and sentiments respecting which you earnestly differed from them and one another. And hereafter, should the exigencies of the country at any time require, Boston cannot lack courageous men, instant in season, who will speak the unwelcome truths which she ought to hear. But the task of to-day, though perhaps not less difficult, is more agreeable. The duty you have imposed upon me, if I rightly apprehend it, is to aid in giving utterance to the feeling which now fills all our hearts. In saying this, I assume that the feeling itself is right; a patriotic joy, exultant with the ecstasies and tender over the agonies of successful war, — a joy full of gratitude for the deliverance already vouchsafed, and causing us to renew our solemn vow that no promise to man, contained in the Declaration of Independence, shall be left unfulfilled.

It has been said of John Adams, that upon the passage of the Resolution of Independence, July 2, 1776, his mind "heaved like the ocean after a storm." Thus does a nation's heart heave to-day. The voice of its thanksgiving is as the voice of many waters. A mystic chord, stretched from our one heart across the intervening years, vibrates responsively to the words of "the colossus in that debate." Our joy seeks the lofty utterance in which he exclaimed, "the day is past. The second day of July, 1776, will be the most memorable epocha in the history of America; to be celebrated by succeeding generations as the great Anniversary Festival, commemorated as the day of deliverance, by solemn acts of devotion to God Almighty, from one end of the continent to the other, from this time forward, forevermore." He adds, "You will think me transported with enthusiasm, but I am not." "Through all the gloom, I can see the rays of light and glory." "You and I may rue," but "posterity will triumph."

"Posterity will triumph." Yes, we stand in the dawn of the day whose glory was foreseen by the Fathers. Now is fulfilled the word which was then spoken. We are the citizens of an independent and regenerated country. We breathe an atmosphere which is invigorating to liberty. Plymouth Rock, so long refused of the builders, has become the corner-

stone of the republic. To-day we nationalize the
prayer for Massachusetts, devoutly saying, "God save
the United States of America!" The ark, to which
we committed our liberties when the flood of Rebellion
came, and from which the dove was sent forth again
and again only to return each time with the olive branch
in her mouth, now rests upon the summits of victory.
And on this most auspicious birthday of the nation, we
are going forth from that ark to build our altar, and
to look on the bow in the clouds, which tells us that
war shall no more deluge our land.

Has it been befitting, hitherto, that we should celebrate the anniversary of the Declaration of Independence? Then it is doubly befitting that we should do
so from this time forth. To those who have rebelled
and been defeated, we do not presume that this propriety will appear. Nor are we anxious to succeed in
meeting their views of the fitness of things. Four
years ago they intimated that we were not prosperous
enough; and to-day, forsooth, we are too prosperous to
keep the feast. Then they ridiculed the solemnity of
which they are now disposed to complain. But loyalty
does not choose treason for her teacher when she goes
to school. As we were hopeful in the day of adversity,
so will we be grateful in the day of triumph. We did
not omit our feast when Freedom was threatened,

nor will we now that Slavery is overthrown. Yet we indulge in no ungenerous exultation. We rejoice not at the discomfiture of our enemies, but in the Salvation of the Republic. We dreaded war with them, knowing that our own blood flowed in their veins. We clung to the common traditions and glory of the past. We were charitable and forbearing almost to the verge of recreancy. And that patience and long suffering are to-day our vantage-ground. We are sure that no malignity mingles with our joy; but only a just indignation, not untinged with pity and grief. We rejoice not that half a continent is laid waste or covered with mourning, but that liberty has taken another step forward in the world. Whatever of tenderness there may be in our hearts, if we were silent in view of what God has wrought, the very stones would cry out.

It has been said by one of our English critics, that we violated the spirit of this festival, when we undertook to put down the Rebellion by force of arms. " Henceforth," was his language, " the observance of the Fourth of July is an unmeaning ceremony." But that conclusion was reached from an inadequate premise. The critic seemed to see only half of what the Declaration of Independence proclaims. Let no one be misled by the name of that immortal paper. Besides the right of revolution, to which the name especially points. the paper itself declares that there is an inalienable right of liberty, which belongs equally to all men. But allowing our critic his premise, what was that right of revolution declared by the Fathers? Was it something that would legitimate the Southern Rebellion? Was it a principle which we violated in putting down that Rebellion by force? The Fathers of the Republic did not believe in wantonly breaking up any form of government. The oppression must be intolerable and morally wrong, and revolt the only available means of redress, in order to justify such a course. Had the national rule become wicked and intolerably oppressive to the South?

Imagine the conspirators at Montgomery saying that " a decent respect to the opinions of mankind required that they should declare the causes which impelled them to the separation." What were those causes, when fairly stated? A golden passage in the first draft of the Declaration had been dropped to please the Southern delegates. At the framing of the Constitution that noble charter was again compromised to bring South Carolina into the Union. Concession after concession was made to the Slave States, and they seized one centre after another of the Federal power. They wielded the Government of the country; and gradually published their design to make it the bulwark and propagandist of barbarism. Would such

2

a statement as this show "a decent respect to the opinions of mankind?" Do we see here any warrant for using that carefully defined Right of Revolution which the Fathers claimed? No, they dared not make an honest appeal to history. Their better nature told them that they could give only the most monstrous of reasons for what they did. Hence the fictions of State Sovereignty and the Right of Secession, by which they sought to escape. The war under Abraham Lincoln hostile to the Declaration of Independence? It was reluctantly accepted to rescue that Declaration from the spoiler. Had we failed to crush the Rebellion, and had foreign powers stooped to the infamy of a full recognition; had we lost everything else, still we should not have lost our fidelity to those rights which the Fathers of the Republic held sacred.

But this is not all. So far from having fallen back, we stand higher to-day than on any previous birthday of the nation. Did the first war with England establish the Right of Revolution? The war for the Union has not yielded that right, but saved it from an infamous abuse. And our time-hallowed festival, while retaining all its earlier meaning, is to-day vastly more significant than ever before. We should feel that we have met to inaugurate a new jubilee of freedom. Those voices of the Declaration which proclaim liberty and equality are no longer muffled. They peal forth clearly in every note of joy, and they fall only upon willing ears. To-day, for the first time, the mighty chorus is entire. Our feast is kept not merely in the oldness of the letter, but in the newness of the spirit. As we are amending the Constitution, so I could wish that we might amend the Declaration, by restoring to it those words which were blotted at the demand of Slavery. " He has waged cruel war against human nature itself, violating its most sacred rights of life and liberty in the persons of a distant people who never offended him, captivating and carrying them into slavery in another hemisphere, or to incur miserable death in their transportation thither. This piratical warfare, the opprobrium of INFIDEL powers, is the warfare of the CHRISTIAN King of Great Britain. Determined to keep open a market where MEN should be bought and sold, he has prostituted his negative for suppressing every legislative attempt to prohibit or to restrain this execrable commerce. And that this assemblage of horrors might want no fact of distinguished die, he is now exciting these very people to rise in arms among us, and to purchase that liberty of which he has deprived them, by murdering the people upon whom he has obtruded them ; thus paying off former crimes committed against the LIBERTIES of one people with crimes which he urges them to commit against the LIVES of another." That is what Jefferson said when he

would show " a decent respect to the opinions of mankind," by stating the causes which impelled the colonies
to declare their independence. For more than fourscore
years that passage has lain rusting, like a sword in its
scabbard. But the malign Power which doomed it to
such ignominy has been overthrown. We draw it
forth to-day, amid the new glory which has risen upon
us. We brandish aloft its reburnished blade, that it
may flash across the sea the double record, — who it
was that planted, and who that has uprooted the institution of American slavery.

Standing upon the higher summits of the Declaration, as we now do, it is natural for us to review the
path by which we have ascended. Homer, carefully
enumerates, in the Second Book of the Iliad, the ships
which bore the Greeks to the Trojan war. And it
would be a serious neglect on this anniversary, did I
fail to name some of the more important events which
have brought us to our present position. The rush
of events since the opening of the last Spring has
indeed been overwhelming. We seem to be looking
over the awful brow of Niagara; and the voice of the
cataract is the only voice that can utter our emotions.
But let us go back from the downfall to the source
of the mighty current, and follow it forward.

The Rebellion had its fountains far away in our

history. The little rills began to flow into each other after the Colonial period, and the large streams thus formed became more and more visible as the question of admitting new States was forced upon the country. At length all these streams of disloyalty were gathered into a single basin; and then it was that we beheld the Lake Superior of treason, spreading itself broadly out in the full daylight, and kissing the bended cheek of England on its farther shore. That was the inland sea, around which we went shuddering throughout the year 1861, vainly expostulating with those who would trust their all to its waters. Before the year had dawned, a weak old man, soon to vacate the high office which he had allowed treason to control, told us, in words that would have appalled our hearts had we been base enough to believe them, that the Rebellion was wrong, and that any forcible resistance of it would also be very wrong. There was nothing to do but stand, through a hundred terrible days, bowed in shame and chafing with a just rage, until the mighty Northwest should reach out its long arm and haul up our starry flag to the height from which it had fallen. That long arm never failed us, and it left the proud symbol floating securely when it vanished suddenly out of sight. But how furious the storm in which the banner went up, and by which it was instantly assailed! The sea of Rebellion, changed to a foaming whirlpool after the first thunderclap at Charleston, swept into its broad circle State after State, senators, judges, churches, a large portion of the Army and Navy, and so much of the public property as could be placed in its way. When our Congress met, on the 4th of July, the usurpation had an army with full ranks, superbly officered, well supplied and drilled, and every branch of its affairs, whether at home or abroad, was in able and experienced hands. Before the first leaves of Autumn fell, we had lost Ellsworth, — the rising star of our volunteer soldiery; Senator Douglas, — from whose position and known loyalty much was expected; Winthrop and Greble, — one a child of genius, the other a true son of Mars; and General Lyon, who, more than any other loyal officer up to that time, had shown the qualities of a great commander. The humiliating battle of Bull Run had been fought, — revealing disloyalty in high places, exposing our ignorance of the art of war, uncovering the approaches to the Capital, and sending a thrill of anguish and terror throughout the land. Later in the season came the surrender of Lexington, — opening Missouri to the foot of the invader; the battle of Ball's Bluff,— costing us the lamented Baker, whose great popularity bound the Pacific to the Atlantic coast as with hooks of steel, and quenching the light in many New England homes; and, toward the going out of the year, came the irreg-

ular capture of Mason and Slidell, and the advice of
the Earl of Derby to the British Government, " that
outward-bound ships should signalize English vessels
that war with America was probable." The attitude
of the Border States had paralyzed the Administration, and divided the sentiment of the North ; Congress
could do little more than save itself from falling a prey
to treason ; feelings of humanity compelled the President to recognize " the Confederacy," so far as to
treat with it for exchange of prisoners ; belligerent
rights, and the moral power of sympathy had already
been secured to it from the leading foreign powers,
Russia, " faithful among the faithless," excepted ; and
pirates were roaming over the high seas, commissioned
by the arch-conspirator Davis, " to sink, burn, and
destroy everything which flew the ensign of the so-
called United States of America."

But this carnival-year of treason was not without its
signs of promise to us. The telegram of Secretary
Dix to the special agent in New Orleans, " if any one
attempts to haul down the American flag, shoot him
on the spot ;" the heroism of Anderson and his devoted comrades ; the sublime response to the first call
for troops, Massachusetts, as of old, leading the van ;
the elastic energy of the nation under the stunning
blow of Bull Run ; the battle of Rich Mountain, sav-
ing to us Western Virginia ; the capture of the forts

at Hatteras Inlet, under Admiral Stringham and General Butler; the glorious achievement of the Navy at
Port Royal, under the lamented Dupont; the stubborn
and bloody fight near Belmont, where General Grant
first gave token of that daring, coolness, modesty, strategy, and invincible nerve, which have since won him
our eternal gratitude; the moral courage and wisdom
of Mr. Seward, in appeasing the wrath of England
over the affair of the " Trent; " these events were all
unmistakable omens that the triumphing of the wicked
would be short.

The huge volume of the Rebellion, thus sensibly
diminished, now shrunk at a rapid rate. The new year
(1862) gave Mason and Slidell to England, by whom
they were " coldly received; " Edwin M. Stanton, the
Cato among our heads of departments, became Secretary of War; the battle of Mill Spring settled the issue
in the Border States; the capture of Forts Henry and
Donelson, and of Roanoke Island, brought the nation
to its feet in a frenzy of delight; Pea Ridge followed,
crushing the Rebel cause in Missouri; then came the
Providential exploit of the first Monitor, swiftly aveng-
ing the loss of the " Congress " and " Cumberland,"
and opening a new era in the history of naval warfare.
On the heels of these victories treads that at Newbern,
confirming our supremacy in Eastern North Carolina;
that at Winchester, where " Stonewall " Jackson was

defeated and driven back; and the terrific struggle of
Pittsburg Landing, where unflinching determination
again prevailed, chiefly through General Sherman, —
"his martial features terrible," then, as ever, the Tela-
monian Ajax of the war. We were puzzled, rather
than made anxious, when we knew that Lee had evac-
uated Manassas; soon the coasts of Georgia and
Florida were ours; General Pope and Commodores
Foote and Davis, had opened the Mississippi far down-
wards; and when New Orleans had surrendered to
Farragut, who found the people there so insolent that
he turned them over to General Butler, in that glad
hour it seemed to us that we could already discern
the angel of peace, his feet beautiful upon the mountains, bringing good tidings, and saying unto us, " Your
God reigneth."

Our God did reign. And because He loved us, He
did not suffer us at that time to triumph. Again the
Rebellion began to unfold its narrowed volume. All
eyes were now fixed upon the Army of the Potomac, —
noblest Army the world has ever seen, — grand at last
with the splendors of victory, as it was grand at first
in the gloom of disaster. Wasted in its slow advance,
after the barren successes at Yorktown and Williams-
burg, it lay, the victim of an invisible destroyer, along
the muddy slopes of the Chickahominy. General
Banks, assailed by the combined forces of Jackson

3

and Ewell, had skilfully withdrawn his little army
from the Valley of the Shenandoah. It was determined that the force under McDowell should cover
Washington, and not the right wing of the Army of
the Potomac. Jackson was thus at liberty to co-operate
with Lee against McClellan, whose plan for falling
back had been discovered by Stuart's famous raid, and
whose difficulties had been increased rather than less-
ened, by the costly victories of Fair Oaks and Mechan-
icsville. The first attempt at withdrawal was the signal
for furious pursuit. But our brave columns, though
vastly outnumbered, were not once beaten in the field.
Their march was not a retreat in the proper sense of
the term; and each time they turned upon the pur-
suing legions of the foe, at Gaines's Mills, the Chickahominy, Peach Orchard and Savage's Station, White
Oak Swamp and Malvern Hill, they sent those legions,
mangled and disheartened, backward. It was not in
the fighting, but through divided counsels, that the
campaign proved a failure. The Army still supposed
itself on the way to Richmond, when the order came
for it to move toward Washington. Then it was that
the Rebellion rolled out its hidden masses. At Cedar
Mountain it struck a blow that darkened many homes
in New England; and this was but the opening of
the series of assaults which culminated in the second
battle of Bull Run, and which swept on until met by

an impassable barrier at South Mountain and Antietam. Nor did the sweep of the Rebellion seem to grow less, but only more vast, at the great battles of Fredericksburg, Murfreesboro,' and Chancellorsville. The elections in the North had been carried against the loyal cause, the assassination of Senator Sumner had been threatened in New York, and the Congress at Richmond had proposed an alliance with the States on the Pacific coast.

But our God was reigning. The school of calamity had opened our eyes to see those four millions of blacks, who everywhere had a welcome for us, and whose forced labors enabled the Rebels to keep their armies in the field. Our Congress, whose achievements for freedom we cannot too much admire, had smoothed the way for the President. With Slavery abolished in the District, and forever shut out from the Territories; with Hayti fully recognized, the Fugitive Slave Law repealed, and the Confiscation Act passed, it was easy for Abraham Lincoln, pressed on by military necessity, to issue that decree of EMANCIPATION which made him the saviour of his country, and of a race of men. Thoughts of foreign interference were now at an end; and Heaven, though trying our faith for a time, at length began to smile. The enlistment of the blacks as soldiers rapidly followed; and to our own Governor Andrew especially is due the high honor of urging that measure forward to complete success. On the fourth of July, 1863, the Rebellion had received its death wound. Vicksburg fell, involving the fall of Port Hudson, and thus opening the Mississippi; and victory settled on our banners at Gettysburg, after a contest which history, as I think, will pronounce the great and decisive battle of the war.

I need not speak of the brave men who there fought. The classic genius of Everett, now immortal, has embalmed their names; and the matchless Eulogy of the Martyr-President, has left nothing for eloquence or poetry to add. Now, upon the failure of the July riots, the Rebellion withdrew into its inmost recesses, knowing that its life depended on keeping out of the way. The battle of Fort Wagner, costing us so dear; and that at Chickamauga, revealing the great commander in General Thomas; and others of less note, in the South and West, did not change the fixed course of events. Grant and Sherman, in their own close counsels, were forecasting the final campaign. General Burnside opened the gates of East Tennessee. The battle of Mission Ridge, and the storming of Lookout Mountain, where Hooker's warriors seemed to wield the artillery of the clouds, secured an open door into Georgia. Deeply pained, but unhindered, by the disaster on Red River, the new regiments rallied on the .

banks of the Rapidan under the Lieutenant-General, and near Chattanooga under his great subordinate. The Rebels were confused and bewildered in their hiding-places, not knowing what the omens foretokened. They comprehended the game only when they had lost it. The movement of Meade's army to the South of Petersburg, so costly but so necessary, and involving such immense sacrifice of life at Spottsylvania, the Wilderness, Laurel Hill, Coal Harbor, and on the banks of James River, closed the iron hand of fate upon the main army of the Rebellion. It was now dangerous for that army to remain stationary, and far more dangerous for it to attempt to move. The defeat of Sigel and Hunter, and the raids near Washington, could not loosen the stubborn hold of Grant. The failure of the assault planned by Burnside, and the pause of Sherman before Atlanta, sent the currency and the heart of the country down to their lowest point notwithstanding the glorious news from the " Kear-sarge," and the anxiety of the Rebels to treat for peace. But had certain politicians at that time read the purpose of the leading generals, they would not have advised the two wings of the Republican party to drop their separate candidates and unite under some com-mon leader ; nor would certain other politicians have voted the war a failure, and clamored for an armistice and a compromise. The grasp upon the throat of the

Rebellion was not relaxed; Sherman resumed his work upon its extremities, hurling the fragments westward to be completely crushed by Thomas at Franklin and Nashville; the bright pennant of Farragut floated victoriously off the harbor of Mobile; and Sheridan's ride in the Valley sealed the fate of the writhing victim. Every life sacrificed by the Southern leaders after that date was a murder. They knew their cause to be hopeless; only their desperate pride sustained them. Victory carried the national election. The fall of Savannah, Charleston, Wilmington, and Goldsboro' was but the effect of a cause that had already operated. They went down like oaks in the still night after the hurricane has swept over them! The mad blows at Hatcher's Run and Fort Stedman, which recoiled so terribly; the quailing before Sheridan's swift squadrons, all the way round from Lynchburg to Five Forks, the utter collapse, when the final word was given, "up boys, and at them," were an overthrow too awful for my poor description. I can but recur to the figure with which I began this recital. The long gathering, the now unfolding and now contracting waters, were forced to the precipice. In the mists rising out of the abyss into which they went thundering down, we saw calmly shining the bright bow of promise; and our awed and swelling hearts could only exclaim, "The Lord God omnipotent reigneth."

How shall I fitly impress you with the grandeur of
this result to our country? Let us first contrast the
opening with the close of the Rebellion. Never before
did treason start up so pompously, and perish so in-
gloriously. At the secession of South Carolina, Mr.
Keitt said: " We have carried the body of this Union
to its last resting-place, and now we will drop the flag
over its grave." But he is in a traitor's gory grave,
and the flag still waves on high. When the conspirators met at Montgomery, Davis said, " the South is
determined to maintain her position, and make all who
oppose her, smell Southern powder, and feel Southern
steel." But that steel and powder are ours to-day, and
Davis — *quantus mutatus ab illo* — smells a gibbet in
the air. Mr. Stephens said, " in the conflict, thus far,
success has been on our side, complete throughout the
length and breadth of the Confederate States. It is
upon [the enslavement of the African race] as I have
stated, our social fabric is firmly planted; and I cannot
permit myself to doubt the ultimate success and full
recognition of this principle throughout the civilized
and enlightened world." But the only response to
that atrocious sentiment, thus far, has been a universal
cry of indignation; and Mr. Stephens now has other
use for his philosophy, in a fortress whose name (Fort
Warren) reminds him of the revered martyr to liberty
on Bunker Hill. After the outrage on Fort Sumter,

the Rebel Secretary of War said, " I will prophesy that the flag which now flaunts the breeze here will float over the dome of the Capitol at Washington before the first of May. Let them try Southern chivalry and test the extent of Southern resources, and it may float eventually over Faneuil Hall itself." The Governor of South Carolina also said, " we have humbled the flag of the United States. It is the first time in the history of this country that the Stars and Stripes have been humbled. It has been humbled, and humbled by the glorious little State of South Carolina." But the flag then " humbled " is exalted at length, and those who rolled the sacrilege as a " sweet morsel " under their tongues, are vagabonds and fugitives in the earth. The fate of all the leaders in the Rebellion gives a new meaning to the words of a king of Israel ; " Let not him that girdeth on his harness boast himself as he that putteth it off." Not only did they sell their birthright, but that which they most feared has come upon them. We recall here the terrible lines of Addison, and, slightly changing them, exclaim : —

> " There *is* some chosen curse,
> Some hidden thunder in the stores of heaven,
> Red with uncommon wrath, to blast the wretch
> Who seeks his greatness in his country's ruin "

The Rebellion begins and ends its career on a stage

where tragedy and comedy struggle together for the mastery. In its final shout, " *Sic semper tyrannis*," we hear its own doom pronounced; and it goes out of history, as the body of the assassin has gone, into the blackness of darkness forever. Around it hangs the memory of its great swelling words; of sacrilege to the bones of the dead; of Fort Pillow massacres, St. Albans raids, yellow-fever plots, and attempts to burn cities full of women and children. A host of skeleton shadows from Libby, Saulisbury, and Andersonville flit above the place of its torment. It forever hears the horror and laughter of the world shouted after it. And if there be any words, in all the circle of literature, which it may fitly utter, they are: " Let the day perish wherein I was born! Let it not be joined unto the days of the year, nor come into the number of the months! Let no joyful voice come therein. Let them curse it that curse the day; let the stars of the twilight thereof be dark."

Respecting the change that has come over the aristocracy of England, I will be very brief. They are eating their own words at a rapid rate; and the wry faces which they make, while " chewing the bitter cud," are our ample revenge. If they can afford to remember the indecent haste with which they listened to the conspirators; with which they threatened war over the affair of the " Trent;" with which they vir-

tually became allies of the Rebellion; we certainly can.
Our disgust is stirred not a little at their eulogy of our
Martyr-President, whom a short time before they had
so insultingly maligned; but if they can afford to
extend such sympathy, we may well keep silent, and
gratefully — *smile*. Lee and Johnston, and Forrest,
and Taylor, and Kirby Smith, having surrendered, of
course the surrender of England follows. Like a certain Confederate General, she " surrenders unconditionally on condition that she is unconditionally
pardoned." The bills are rather large after that little
pleasantry of the " Alabama." Our portly friend pro-
tests that he didn't steal the butter and put it in his
hat; and therefore, though something very much *like*
butter is streaming down his glowing cheeks, yet, if he
says he didn't, possibly he didn't. We mean that our
memory shall be as short as England's; that is, we will
forget the hostility of the titled few, and remember the
sympathy of the untitled many among her subjects.

As for France and Mexico, we cannot forget the
exposed heel of Achilles; and we shall take care that
no Paris, with poisoned arrow, wounds us to death on
our Southwestern border.

It might be thought ungenerous to contrast our
present feelings with those of the vanquished; let us
therefore remember how we felt at the outbreak of
the Rebellion, and from the contrast thus suggested

learn the greatness of our cause for rejoicing. We
shall never forget that Saturday on which Sumter
fell, nor the Sunday next following. Least of all
shall we ever forget the Sunday next following the
massacre of our loyal soldiers in Baltimore. Sabbaths
we cannot call those days, for they brought no rest to
us. We were astounded, bewildered, appalled. We
went unto the house of God, only to calm ourselves
there under His great shadow, as we looked forth on
the gathering tempest of war. Then we gazed down
a horrible vista of devastation, famine, tears, blood,
and wild disorder. We looked, "And behold a pale
horse; and his name that sat on him was Death, and
Hell followed with him." We saw the iron-hoofed
demon of war,— his neck clothed with thunder, pawing
in the valleys, displaying the glory of his nostrils,
swallowing the ground with fierceness and rage, saying
among the trumpets, "Ha, ha!" smelling the battle, the
thunder of the captains, and the shouting; we saw this
mighty waster going forth to trample down all our beautiful civilization, to fill every house in the land with
mourning, to turn the moon into blood, and cast the stars
unto the ground like untimely figs. But lo. the vision is
changed! Another angel has sounded, even the angel
of peace. We look up, and, behold, all the *stars* are
in their places. Their bands have not been loosed nor
their sweet influence disowned.

"The terrible steed lies with nostril all wide,
  And through it there rolls not the breath of his pride."

Yes, the gloom and horror are behind us, and the glory before. We lay aside the spirit of heaviness, and put on the bright apparel of joy. For He that now cometh — escorted by our returning conquerors — is meek and lowly. His coming is as showers upon the mown grass. We see waste places rejoicing at His approach, the wilderness budding and blossoming, the rose growing again in Sharon, the lily reappearing in the valley, the hills clothed with flocks and corn and the free floods clapping their hands. Up, come ye, let us spread our garments in the way; let us cut down branches, and strew them before this King of Peace! Let us go before, and follow after, and sing, " Be ye lifted up, ye everlasting doors." Let the children, also, with their glad hosannas, swell our chorus of welcome. For Peace cometh, crowned with war's victories, to sway a benign sceptre over the land.

Only a little more than four years ago we were bringing home, from the bloody pavement in Baltimore, our young soldiers, slain for rushing between the raised dagger of treason and the nation's life. Sorrowful indeed was that funeral; for the air was thick with startling omens, and the tidings, coming on every pulse of the electric wires, smote us like the sirocco's

breath. But to-day the grave of those martyrs is holy
ground. You have recently made a pilgrimage to
their sculptured monument, going with songs of joy,
and with garlands in your hands, to tell to a thousand
generations that Liberty does not forget, in the day of
her triumph, those "who made their lives an offering" for her sake. A little more than four years
ago all our hearts were on board the "Star of the
West," sailing into Charleston harbor, carrying food
to a little band of starving men; only to be warned
back by a hostile shot, and to be forced to look on, in
powerless indignation and shame, while the encircling
batteries of treason vomited forth their inhuman fury
upon that small and fainting company; until the stars
of our nationality went down, insulted but not dishonored. into the smoke and flames of fratricidal war.
But lo, the change! A rod out of heaven has touched
and transfigured the scene. Since the magnolias last
bloomed, all our hearts have been on board another
ship, bearing upon it some of the scarred veterans of
freedom, and with them the heroic Anderson, who
carried with him the same starry Symbol that first
went down. This they lifted up to its former proud
height. amid shoutings, the sobbings of joy, jubilant
music, and thunders of loyal cannon. And thus was
proclaimed, to all traitors, and the enemies of liberty
everywhere, that the covenant which makes these

States a nation is an everlasting bond; and that their
Union — by the sweet ministries of peace, if possible,
but, if necessary, by the thunderbolts of war — " must
and shall be preserved." No vain boasting, no empty
exultation, no vulgar triumph over the vanquished,
but a solemn admonition to us and our children, and to
all the world, that " whosoever falleth on this rock
shall be broken, and on whomsoever it falleth it shall
grind him to powder ! "

But I proceed to some of the more lasting results
of the war. Of its effect as realizing the spirit of
the Declaration I have already spoken.

The triumph of our loyal arms has settled the question of sovereignty, as between the Union and the
several States. It was said of the States of ancient
Greece, that they lost their government by desiring
severally to govern: *Greciæ civitates, dum imperare
singulæ cupiunt, imperium omnes perdiderunt.* A similar
fate threatened the American Republic, growing out of
the heresy of State Sovereignty. But the war is at an
end, and where are those Sovereign States ? Do they
appear, to negotiate a peace with the Federal Government? No; they cannot shield the assailants of
the Union and Constitution. Those assailants find,
as Roman traitors once found, that " they must answer
at the bar of the assembly as criminals, not pretend to

negotiate with the Republic as equals." The States are but municipalities; in the government of the whole country is vested the sovereign power. We have heard of treason against a State; but we now see that such a crime is always relative to the Union. No State, acting primarily and independently, defines the crime of treason and prescribes its penalty; it exercises that function only by virtue of its connection with the United States. Robert E. Lee, fancying the authority of Virginia paramount to that of the Republic, became a traitor; Andrew Johnson, true to his primary rather than his secondary allegiance, maintained his loyalty. " But if the question of sovereignty was not settled before the war, and if Lee honestly believed Virginia to be sovereign, ought he to suffer the penalty of treason?" Certainly not for that simple belief. But he went further. He did that which he had often seen defined as treason in the Constitution of his country. Let no one be punished for believing the abstract doctrine of State Sovereignty; but let those who have made war upon the United States, and the whole country through them, be taught the horrible nature of their crime. Treason, as we now perceive, is not properly an offence against Massachusetts, or Virginia; not the killing of a public servant, however high his office; but an attempt to murder the sovereignty of the people of the United States. No other crime can compare with it in guilt. It is not merely hurling a single planet from its sphere, but destroying the power of gravitation itself. Thank God, the thin pretext, from which so many have leaped into bloody Rebellion, is no more! Like the gourd of Jonah, it has perished with the night in which it grew up. All the people of the land know now, that in case of collision between civil authorities, they owe a single paramount allegiance; and that they owe it to the Government whose organic law defines high treason, and declares that Congress shall determine its penalty.

The triumphant issue of the war has proved the power of an elective government to cope with armed Rebellion. Heretofore, the advocates of hereditary power have said, " Your government by the people, with universal suffrage and a change of rulers every four years, may do very well on a small scale, and while you are held together by the necessity of making common cause against other nations. But wait till you have a broad territory, and many competing interests among your citizens: and then, in case of any considerable revolt, see how soon your country will go to pieces. Your Government, resting as it does on the shoulders of the masses, will have for its chief managers men of inferior ability; the brief tenure of office will not train great leaders; your ablest men, seeing themselves but units in the mass, will lack patriotism;

in any threatening emergency, your nation will find itself unprepared." This reasoning was so plausible, and in part so philosophical, that some of us half believed it. Our hearts misgave us when we knew that certain of the States were banded together to destroy our Government. There did seem to be a want of patriotism among our ablest men; there was a lack of trained leaders; we were wofully unready to cope with the Rebellion. But one element in our favor, outweighing all the advantages of a monarchy, had been too much overlooked. The people knew that the Government was their government. and its cause their cause. If it was dishonored, they were dishonored; if it was lost. their earthly hopes were lost. No sophistries could blind them to the momentous issue. Hence the rush to arms. Hence the cheerful submission to taxes, and other necessary burdens and restraints. Hence the readiness to loan the nation whatever treasure it might need. Our first efforts were awkward and unsuccessful; and, of those whom we tried as leaders, one after another failed. But the resources were vast; the determination to conquer grew more stern; gradually we learned how; and those who wished us evil, and our own doubting hearts, were taught that what a free people *wills* it can perform. We have shown that the humblest man, if honest, can be the successful ruler of the mightiest nation on the

5

globe. The people are too intelligent, too much disposed to justice and public order, to need intellectual giants in the chairs of state. The wolf, and the bear, and the lion have been subdued to the habits of the lamb and the ox; " and a little child may lead them." The spirit of the people has made our rulers great. All fears respecting the stability of such a government as ours are forever dispelled. There is, in the nation, a centripetal power balancing its centrifugal power; it may be as permanent as it is beneficent, as strong as it is free. Hitherto our Republic has been called an experiment; it will be called so no longer. Royalists know this. They see that the weapon with which they have thus far defended their kings is wrested from them. They are asking themselves, with blanched cheeks, what they have done and said to us in the day of our trouble.

Let me here give way a moment to the mouth-piece of the English aristocracy. Hear it: " It has been vulgarly supposed that democracy is necessarily incompatible with strength and vigor of executive action, and that the concentration of power in a single despot is necessary for the conduct of a great war. That delusion the American struggle has dispelled. It has been thought that democracies were necessarily fickle to their rulers, unstable and wavering in their determination. That, too, the democracy of America has disproved. It has been said that democracies were necessarily violent and cruel in their disposition, and that from impatience of discipline and obedience they are unapt for military success. No man can say that now. It has been said that democracies would not support the expenses of war and the burdens of taxation. This is proved not to be the case. No autocrat that the world has ever seen, has received a more firm and unbounded support, and commanded more unlimited resources than those which the American people have freely placed at the disposal of Mr. Lincoln. His re-election in 1864 was evidence of the wise and prudent firmness of the people who exercised the suffrage. and the result ought to have left no doubt on the minds of thoughtful men as to the necessary issue of the great contest." Comment is needless. To such language every American patriot says, as the friend of Antonio said to Shylock —

" I thank thee, Jew, for giving me that word ! "

The war has also proved that we are in no danger from military ambition. The soldiers of Cæsar and Napoleon were ready to follow their adored commanders in any attempt at usurpation. Not so our soldiers. They know what they have been suffering and fighting for ; for a Government which belongs to themselves, and which not even their most admired general, for whom they would die any moment, can be permitted in the smallest particular to usurp or disown. Thank God, the American people are able to discriminate in their gratitude. No renown of the warrior can so dazzle them as to make them forget the proper subordination of the military to the civil power. Henceforth we shall be less nervous at popular admiration lavished on the successful general. It is not the blind applause of an unthinking populace, but thanks rendered to one who is expected to be a benefactor in the future as well as in the past. We are deeply grieved that it has cost the hero of Atlanta so dear, or that any other hero's tripping should be the price of this valuable lesson; and we are and always will be grateful to the man who could say to his troops, as Sherman did, in bidding them adieu after all that had happened, " be good citizens in peace as you have been good soldiers in war."

Another result of the struggle has been to strengthen, rather than shake, the foundation of our liberties. The essential theory of the Government is not changed, but confirmed and made to operate on a larger scale. It is an axiom of history that civil wars are ended only by compromise. That axiom has failed for once. The rebellions of England have revolutionized her government, though nominally it is much the same. When kings come out of wars with their subjects, they never after sit as firmly as before on their thrones. They must humor the people, and yield more or less of the reality for the sake of the semblance of power. But our Government has not yielded anything to the Rebels yet. and will be guilty of a foolish act if it ever does. Its basis is broader and deeper to-day than when the war began. The people understand its spirit better, and are wedded to it by a more determined loyalty. The great problems forced upon their attention, have taught them their duties and revealed to them their rights. And the Institution with which they might have been tempted to compromise has ceased to exist. Was the way of the wicked ever more utterly turned upside down? The attempt was to assassinate Liberty; the result is that Slavery has been cast into an ignominious grave. The attempt was to rivet the chains of bondage on a race of men; the result is that they are and ever shall be free. The attempt was to carry a monstrous wrong upward to our Northern border; the result is that freedom and the right have been carried downward to our Southern border. This is a new feature in the history of rebellions. It teaches us that they " fight against the stars in their courses " who fight against the rights of man; that, as under the throne so upon the throne, the march of human liberty is forever onward, When it rises up none can hinder, and when it strikes none can stand.

The war has also deepened the affection of the people for the Union, in all parts of the land. The suffering and glory it has occasioned are a common heritage. The East and West can never forget that they have stood shoulder to shoulder throughout the terrible struggle — that they have rejoiced together over the same victories, and wept together over the same reverses. The blood of their sons has flowed together on a hundred battle-fields, and those sons are now sleeping side by side in the soldier's grave. Nor do we doubt that the era of wiser counsels and kindlier feeling, is coming to the people of the South; when they also, having learned the real cause of their troubles, shall reach forth a fraternal hand unto those who have broken the yoke ofan Oligarchy from off their necks. Yes, it is our country; our one country; our redeemed and renovated country, that every American heart embraces to-day. We of the East can never resign our share in the glory of Sherman's army, and they of the West will ever claim that the army which conquered Lee was theirs. No patriot, from the Mississippi to the Pacific Coast, will ever admit to himself that the tomb of Abraham Lincoln is in a foreign country; and we who have " seen his star in the East " can never endure a strange flag waving over that shrine, as we go thither, with our sweet spices, to remember whom he loved and for whom he was offered.

I will name but one other result of the war, itself an effect of the results already named. The question of Sovereignty settled, the power of cohesion in a free government proved, and the Republic raised to leadership among the nations, our character as a people will naturally improve. Not that the American people have been especially bad, but they are in a condition to grow better. The consciousness of power begets a feeling of repose. It gives steadiness and self-poise to both nations and men. If Southern " chivalry " had been more genuine, it would have boasted less. If our country had been more truly " the home of the free," the shouts for freedom would have been less noisy. Those friends abroad who expect that we shall be made vain-glorious and insolent by our success, are mistaken. Being sure of our position, we shall lose our sensitiveness, and grow calmer and more self-possessed. Our nationality is vindicated. Other governments, contemptuous once, now look toward us with respect and fear. But their fear is groundless, so long as their treatment of us is just. The war has not made us a military people ; but only shown that when we *must* fight we fight through to victory. Standing on our high places, we shall not breathe out slaughter against other nations, but the rather overlook their impotent unfriendliness. This new dignity will be promotive of peace everywhere. It will bring forth in us more of

the fruits of manly virtue. Ceasing to fear criticism,
we shall be less criticized. The opinions of foreigners
will not disturb us much hereafter. We shall learn to
be content, and modestly proud, in the enjoyment of
our own history, our own institutions, our own simple
manners and customs. It is respectable now to be a
citizen of the United States, — respectable anywhere.
We have only to keep quietly in our place. We have
a character, and that character will give a charm to
American life. Those who have taunted us hitherto
will henceforth treat us with deference. They will find
a new merit in our literature, a new refinement in our
society, — grace and dignity where all was vulgar and
trivial before. We shall learn that success, as well as
a good deed, shines very far " in a naughty world,"
that it transforms a nation of plebeians into a nation of
patricians, that it changes the worthless into the " most
worshipful." Heretofore America has imitated Europe;
hereafter Europe will imitate America. And the influence of this new treatment, instead of puffing us up,
will beget in us all a sober self-respect. It will render
us a calmer people; will make us content with our
citizenship, and all the simple republican customs
bequeathed to us. Thus shall the most lasting, the
grandest, the richest result of the mighty struggle be
secured.

I now come to the most grateful, and withal the tenderest portion of my task. It is the offering of our united thanks unto those who have achieved for us the priceless boon. Soldiers from the Army and Navy, once soldiers but now again citizens, we hail you to-day as our benefactors and deliverers. We welcome you home from the fatigues of the march, the wearisome camp, and the awful ecstacy of battle. Through four terrible years you have looked without quailing on the ghastly visage of war. You have patiently borne the heats of Summer and the frosts of Winter. You have cheerfully exchanged the delights of home for the hardships of the campaign or blockade. Not only the armed foe, but the wasting malaria has lurked along your resistless advance. You know the agony and the transport of the deadly encounter. How many times, standing each man at his post, in the long line of gleaming sabres and bayonets, every hand clenched and every eye distended, you have caught the peal of your leader's clarion, and sprung through the iron storm to the embrace of victory! But all that has passed away. The mangled forests are putting on an unwonted verdure. the fields once blackened by the fiery breath of war are now covered with their softest bloom, and the vessels of commerce are riding on all the national waters. The carnage, the groans, the cries for succor, the fierce onset and sullen recoil, the thunders of the

6

artillery, and the missiles screaming like demons
in the air, have given way to pæans, civic processions and songs of thanksgiving. The flag of your
country, so often rent and torn in your grasp, and
which you have borne to triumph again and again,
over the quaking earth or through the hurricane of
death in river and bay, rolls out its peaceful folds
above you, every star blazing with the glory of your
deeds, in token of a nation's gratitude. We come forth
to greet you, — sires and matrons, young men and
maidens, children and those bowed with age ; to own
the vast debt which we can never pay, and to say, from
full hearts, " We thank you, God bless you ! "

But while we thus address you, you are thinking of
the fallen. With a soldier's generosity you wish they
could be here to share in the thrice-earned welcome.
Possibly they are here, from many a grave in which
you laid them after the strife ; pleased with these festivities, and with the return of joy to the nation, but far
above any ability of ours either to bless or to injure.
You may tarnish your laurels, or an envious hand may
pluck them from you. But your fallen comrades are
exposed to no such accident. They are doubly fortunate, for the same event which crowned them with
honor has placed them beyond the possibility of losing
their crown. Many of them died in the darkest hours
of the Republic ; others in the early dawn of peace,

while " the morning stars were singing together." But
victory and defeat make no differences among them
now. They all have conquered in the final triumph.
Their names will alike thrill the coming ages, as loftily
spoken by the tongues of the eloquent; and their
deeds will forever be chanted by immortal minstrels.
They were together " brave men, who repose in the
public monuments, all of whom alike, as being worthy
of the same honor, the country buried, not alone the
successful or victorious; and justly, for the duty of
brave men was done by all, their fortune being such as
God assigned to each."

> " By fairy hands their knell is rung,
> By forms unseen their dirge is sung;
> There Honor comes, a pilgrim gray,
> To bless the turf that wraps their clay;
> And Freedom shall awhile repair,
> To dwell a weeping hermit there."

And ye know, departed soldiers of the Republic, that
your President was a partaker in your " last full measure of devotion." Yes, you have him, for you deserve
him more than we. Have you left many widows on
the earth? Among them the wife of Abraham Lincoln
is one. Are your fatherless children now waiting for
us to pay over to them a little of the great debt we
owe? Among them the children of Abraham Lincoln

mourn a father gone to be with you. The man so
exalted, whose summons drew you from happy homes
to be offered on the altars of war, has himself followed
in the sacrificial column. His mortal form is laid as
low as yours. It can no longer be said that he called
you to a death which did not threaten him. O, ye
sightless couriers of the air, waiting around that new-
made sepulchre at Springfield, take up this truth — the
invisible Republic where President and people still are
one — and bear it abroad on gentle wings, and reveal it
tenderly to every poor heart that bemoans a husband,
or son, or friend, or brother slain! In the words of an
ancient orator, " It becomes us to honor the dead, and
to lament the living. For what pleasure, what consola-
tion remains to them? They are deprived of those
who love them, but who preferring virtue to every connection, have left them fatherless, widowed and forlorn.
Of all their relations, the children, too young to feel
their loss, are least to be lamented ; but most of all the
parents, who are too old ever to forget it. They nourished and brought up children to be the comforts of
their age, but of these, in the decline of life, they are
deprived, and with them of all their hopes. We shall
best honor the dead, then, by extending our protection
to the living. We must assist and defend their widows,
protect and honor their parents, embrace and cherish
their orphans. Who deserve more honor than the

dead? Who are entitled to more sympathy than their
kindred?"

Nor in the field alone, has the meed of a nation's
thanks been earned. At home the fair have toiled and
waited for the brave. The flame on the altar of Hymen,
which has burnt low while there was sterner work to
do, will be kindled afresh at the return of the saviours
of the country. The Soldiers' Aid Societies, the San-
itary and Christian Commissions, and the records of all
our military hospitals, are an eternal monument to
woman's patriotism and woman's love. And as, in the
past, they have chosen to be widows of brave men
rather than the wives of cowards, so now, neither scar
nor crutch, nor artificial limb, will damage the suit of
those who deserve the fair. Soldiers, while we applaud
your heroism, there is also due, from you, a recognition
of services by those who have not stood at the front.
As I am enough of a civilian to speak their gratitude
to you, so I have been enough of a soldier to return
thanks in your name to them. They have exerted
themselves to the utmost that you might lack no per-
sonal comfort, and that the sinews of war might ever
be tense and strong. And as the various classes of
loyal citizens look around upon one another to-day, each
esteeming others better than himself, perhaps the truest
word we can utter is that the whole loyal people of the

land, wherever any may have struggled or toiled, are
the real and the only chief hero of the war.

We cannot forget, in this glad hour, how much we
owe to the patriotic statesmen of former days. The
noble record of the last two Congresses is but the carrying forward of what their predecessors had begun.
We remember the perils and speak gently of the mis-
takes, while we admire what we will believe was the
purpose of those men. It is not in our hearts to doubt
on which side of the line of battle Rufus Choate would
have stood, had he lived to see that line clearly drawn.
In no man was the sentiment of nationality ever more
intense than in him. "The Union broken up?" we
can hear him exclaim with that preternatural voice of
his, "never, while there's enough of Plymouth Rock
left to make a gun flint of!" This whole bloody war
has been but the old battle between Webster and Calhoun, fought through with other weapons and on a
broader stage. Their thoughts have sped from the
mouths of contending cannon, their words have clashed
in the fierce shock of encountering steel. Their spirits
have struggled in the air while loyalty and treason
were struggling on the plain below. They have shud-
dered or smiled, as each one has seen his idea smitten
down or winning the day. And when the final acclaim
of the armies of the Union went up, could we not
almost see the sullen ghost of Calhoun turning away

into the darkness? Could we not again hear Webster's voice coming to us in the grand music of the ocean, across his tomb at Marshfield, and saying, "the aspiration of my life is attained? I now *do* behold the gorgeous ensign of the Republic known and honored throughout the earth; full high advanced, its arms and trophies streaming in *more* than their original lustre, not a stripe erased nor a star obscured; and everywhere, spread all over in characters of living light, blazing on all its ample folds, as they float over the sea and over the land, and in every wind under the whole heaven, there *is* emblazoned that sentiment, dear to every American heart — Liberty and Union, now and forever, one and inseparable."

You will not deem it merely a professional act in me, my friends, if I remind you that to God is due our supreme gratitude to-day. This obligation you have recognized in the service of prayer. The war has renewed our faith in a Divine Providence controlling the destinies of nations, and without which not a sparrow falleth. His throne has rested firmly on the vexed sea of Rebellion, and He has wielded all its wrath for our complete deliverance. In the first shot at Sumter we heard the voice of God saying, " arise, my people ; " and in the last shot at Ford's Theatre we saw Him delivering over the sword of justice into the hands of one who believes that " treason is a crime,

and not merely difference of opinion." All along He
has sent us defeats when our cause needed them.
Many a deliverance has been so unexpected, and from
sources so new and strange, that we could only say,
"it is the Lord's doing;" nor did He permit the
crowning success to come until liberty had been
assured to all the inhabitants of the land.   Perhaps
there is no pious word on record, more expressive of
what we should feel to-day, than Admiral Farragut's
order after the taking of New Orleans: "Eleven
o'clock this morning is the hour appointed to return
thanks to Almighty God for his great goodness and
mercy.   At that hour the church pennant will be
hoisted on every vessel of the fleet, and their crews
assembled, will, in humiliation and prayer, make their
acknowledgments therefor, to the Great Dispenser of
all human events."   Following this bright example,
and that of many loyal governors and brave generals,
and of our departed and our living President, — nay,
indeed, speaking from the deep impulse of our own
thankful hearts, — it is unto the Lord that we sing our
new song, for he it is that hath done marvellous
things : "His right hand and His holy arm have got-
ten Him the victory."

Let it not be inferred, from the tenor of these
remarks, that I see no peril in the future. What shall

be the treatment of the disloyal, and what the basis of citizenship in the reconstructed States, are questions of grave concern.

Are we exhorted to be kind to the Rebels? That appeal is needless. We shall be kind to them. Many of us have very tender reasons for treating them kindly. We always have been kind to them; erring on that side, and yielding to their unjust demands, until they inferred that we could not be aroused to maintain our rights. We may accept it as an axiom, that the people of the North cannot be cruel towards the leaders in the South. All our danger, then, is on the other side. Let us not give other nations occasion to say that we make a commodity of justice. Let not the offenders themselves despise us for fearing to vindicate the majesty of the Republic. Will good citizens feel altogether safe, in our country, if it is to have admired Rebels roaming at large in all parts of it for a generation to come? Let us not be so kind to the disloyal as to be unkind to the loyal. Should not those in the South who have fought on our side be cared for before those who have fought against us? Those who have been true to the Government should be protected first. This is justice, whose claims are sacred. Nor is it magnanimity, but a crime which nature abhors, to cherish enemies who are outraging our friends. Shall we leave the blacks in the power

7

of the exasperated foe, knowing, as we do, that the savage spite which cannot touch us will be wreaked upon their unsheltered heads? I shall believe that the revolt of the rebel angels has succeeded, and that Satan now sits on the throne of God, if such horrible treachery can exist and go unscourged of heaven! While the Saviour of men was riding in triumph to Jerusalem, "He beheld the city, and wept over it." But those tears did not prevent Him from saying, " Behold your house is left unto you desolate." Imitating that divine act to-day, we raise our bitter cry over prostrate treason, even while we call on Justice to draw out her sharp sword. There is no malignity in our hearts, but a reverent prayer that the sovereignty of the nation may be magnified and made honorable. *They would have it so.* They trampled on our forbearance and warnings, and defied the power which should be " a terror to evil doers." Let justice be done without the least over doing. Let their doom be so reasonable that no wicked sympathy shall dare to lift its head. Let them be put where no " foreign correspondent" can glorify them ; where no unfriendly court can make use of them ; where no lying pens of their own can fill the world with histories of their treason disguised as patriotism, and of their attempt to nationalize barbarism painted as a struggle for human liberty. Let them be so punished that their example can never prove contagious, and be buried where the bloodhounds of despotism can never scent their graves !

Two acts of the struggle for liberty in America are past ; the third and consummating act is now upon us. The first act closed under Washington, when the Colonies were acknowledged to be free and independent States ; the second act closed under Lincoln, with the vindication of the sovereignty of the Union ; the third act will close when equal political rights are conceded to all men. God grant that the last act may not, like the first two, deluge the land with blood ! May the evil tree be plucked up in the hour of its weakness, before its roots have undergrown and its branches overspread the Republic. The Emancipation Proclamation was but incidental to the war for the Union. Not in the purpose of man, but by the arrangement of God, it has knocked off the chains of the slave. And it has done a negative, rather than a positive work. It has delivered the blacks from chattel slavery, but it has not introduced them into civil liberty. How this last act shall be achieved is the problem now forced upon the country. Our statesmen cannot evade it if they would ; it is taxing their wisdom beyond any other question of the hour ; and whoever solves it successfully will complete the grand American triumvirate. We could wish that the triumvirate, when full, might read —

Washington, Lincoln, Johnson. Do any say that it is inconsistent to demand citizenship for the blacks in the States now returning to the Union, while in many of the so-called Free States only the whites are admitted to the ballot? But the people of these latter States have not rebelled. Security for the future may require of disloyal communities what should not be exacted of the loyal. Only those who have broken the peace are put under bonds to keep the peace. " But the question of suffrage belongs to the States." So it does, while they are in their normal condition. Perhaps the day of military necessity is over; but is there not a necessity of state quite as pressing, which, if not yielded to, will ultimately become a military necessity? If you cannot do a righteous deed for its own sake, yet doing it to prevent war is better statesmanship than waiting for the war to come. A free government can be said to fulfil its purpose only when no class of persons under it has wrongs to be redressed. Emancipation is but a mockery of the blacks, especially while among their late masters, if they be not admitted to citizenship. Perhaps it did not occur to Mr. Lincoln, perhaps he thought it unwise at the time, to make his Proclamation perfect by adding to it: "And, that the promises herein contained may not prove illusory in the end, I do also proclaim, and cause to be published and proclaimed, that,

in reconstructing the State governments now disor-
ganized, the blacks shall be admitted to all the rights
of freemen on the same conditions with the whites."
How much present anxiety would have been prevented
by some such golden clause ! But we will believe that
the question is in safe hands. Surely the Congress, if
made wise by the events of the past, will not " guarantee
a republican form of government" to any State, while
there is manifestly, in that State, a spirit hostile to the
very principles of republicanism. To the loyalty, wisdom, and patriotism of our statesmen we confide this
grave concern. They alone can decide it peacefully ;
and may God have them in his holy keeping !

Anticipating the gradual solution of all remaining
difficulties, in a manner which shall fulfil the hopes of
a generous patriotism, I see, before our country, a
future too grand for my feeble portrayal; a development
of the resources of nature, a growth of manufactures,
a commerce, civilization, and Christianity, which shall
be the glory of the New World and the wonder of the
Old. No man, standing at the sources of the Amazon,
can bring within the range of his vision all its mighty
course from the mountains to the sea ; — its broad
tributaries with their interlacing streams ; its silent
advance through primeval forests, and vaster sweep
across luxuriant savannas ; the sails of adventurers,
and of scientific explorers, moving up into its alluring

mystery; the inexhaustible wealth of field and mine to which it is a natural highway; the current, so like an ocean, with which it proudly yields at last to the ocean's embrace.   And so, standing to-day by the sources of this new stream in American history, we cannot foresee all its unfolding volume; its distant greatness, and grandeur, and majesty; the destinies, mortal and immortal, of both nations and individuals, which it will gather upon its ample bosom, and bear onward and onward, into the unbounded hereafter. We can only lift up our overflowing hearts toward Him whose rod has brought the water out of the rock, and ask that He would direct its wondrous course; draining the richness of all the civilizations into it, and causing it to bless the ages through which it shall roll, until it mingles in that sea of latter-day glory, whose law is peace, and whose tides and waves are the pulsations of a perfect love.

THE CELEBRATION.

THE CELEBRATION.

The Committee of the City Council for making the necessary arrangements to celebrate the eighty-ninth anniversary of the Declaration of American Independence, July 4, 1865, was appointed February 18, and consisted of Aldermen John S. Tyler, Geo. W. Messinger, L. Miles Standish, Charles F. Dana, Geo. W. Sprague, Nathaniel C. Nash, and Edward F. Porter; Councilmen Wm. B. Fowle, John Miller, W. W. Elliott, N. J. Bean, Wm. W. Warren, Joseph Allen, F. W. Palfrey, John P. Ordway, S. H. Loring, J. C. Haynes, S. B. Stebbins, M. W. Richardson, and Sumner Crosby.

By invitation of the Committee, His Honor Mayor Lincoln was invited to consult with them, and to act with and for them on public occasions. Before the time had arrived for making definite and precise preparations for the celebration, the War came to an end, and it was considered on all hands that the Fourth of July ought to be signalized by demonstrations of joy even more extensive than have heretofore been customary. The appropriation was accordingly increased by the City Council, and the Committee devoted themselves to perfecting a programme of celebration which would gratify all classes and suit all proper tastes. The elements marred the full success of some

8

of the entertainments, but, as a whole, it is believed the celebration was satisfactory to the public, and a fit exposition of the prevalent happy state of feeling in the community.

According to custom, the bells were rung at sunrise, noon, and sunset, and salutes were fired upon the Common, by Capt. French's 2d Battery, at the same hours.

DECORATIONS.

The City Hall, and other public buildings and places were decorated freely with flags, mottoes, shields, &c. From the line crossing Chauncy Street was suspended a shield, bearing on one side the motto: "The security of the American Republic rests in the equality of human rights." (Reverse side.) "God bless the Union! It is dearer to us for the blood of our brave men shed in its defence." At the entrance to the Common, by Park Street, a large and beautiful banner motto was suspended. On the front side was the motto: "We exult that a Nation has not fallen." On one side of this motto was a figure of Justice, with the scales, &c. On the other side the Goddess of Liberty. On the reverse side of this banner a motto: "A new birth of Freedom," with the figure '65 underneath, flanked by a representation of the soldier and sailor. A similar banner, with the following mottoes, was at the Boylston and Charles streets entrance: "One Flag — One Government." (Reverse.) "The Union, it must be preserved."

On Beacon Street Mall, where tables were set for a collation to the "Veteran Soldiers," for nearly 350 feet, flags and other bunting were extended on both sides, and up into the trees, in such a manner as to create a very picturesque effect. At the entrance, opposite Walnut Street, was a large canvas shield, bearing the motto : —

" Honor to the gallant defenders of the Star-Spangled Banner."

Nearer the foot of the Mall was another shield, on which were the mottoes : " What the fathers gained in blood may the sons preserve by virtue !" and " Liberty and Union, one and indivisible, now and forever !"

There was also attached to the trees bordering this display of bunting the names — Abraham Lincoln, Grant, Sherman, Hooker, Burnside, Hancock, Howard, and Sedgwick, on one side of the Mall, and on the opposite were the following names in similar order : Richmond, Vicksburg, Shenandoah Valley, Knoxville, Antietam, Wilderness, Petersburg, Fredericksburg, Gettysburg, and Chancellorville.

The following mottoes were hung at the places designated, with flags : —

Across Winter Street, at Music Hall : —

" Indemnity for the past and security for the future ; the noblest indemnity and the strongest security ever won, because founded in the redemption of a race."

Reverse side — " All honor to the Army and Navy of the United States. Animated by a love of their country, they went forward at its call, and have reaped what they well deserved — the Nation's gratitude."

Across Merchants Row from Faneuil Hall to Market : —

" I leave you, hoping that the lamps of Liberty will burn in your bosoms until there shall no longer be a doubt that all men are created free and equal."— ABRAHAM LINCOLN.

Reverse side — " All honor to the Citizen Soldiers of Massachusetts! In the War for Independence in 1776, and in the War for Freedom in 1861, foremost to defend and prompt to shed their blood in support of man's inalienable right to life, liberty, and the pursuit of happiness."

Across Washington Street from Boston Theatre : —

" Washington promulgated our principles — Warren died in their defence. We intend to perpetuate them."

Reverse side — " The memories of the fathers are the inspirations of her sons."

A MORNING CONCERT

was given upon the Common, at 7 o'clock in the morning, and was listened to with apparent gratification by many thousand people. The musicians numbered eighty, under the direction of Mr. B. A. Burditt, and the pieces played were as follows : —

Hail Columbia.
Russian National Hymn.
Medley of Popular Airs.
England's National Hymn.
Dirge in Memory of President Lincoln.
Hallelujah Chorus.
French National Air.
Ireland's National Air.
German Fatherland.
Our Country's National Airs.
Old Hundred.

THE CHILDREN'S CELEBRATION.

Musical and other entertainments, chiefly for the children of the Public Schools, were provided during the day at Music Hall, Andrews Hall, and the Boston Theatre. These entertainments were under the management of a Committee of the Warren Street Chapel, subject to the directions of the Subcommittee on Children's Celebrations. At the Music Hall, before and after the Oration, at 9, 3½, and 5½ o'clock, three National Organ Concerts were given by Mr. G. E. Whiting and Mrs. L. S. Frohock. At Andrews Hall, at 9, 11, 1, 3, and 5 o'clock, there were exhibitions of natural magic, legerdemain, ventriloquism, and Punch and Judy, by Henry Bryant. At the Boston Theatre there was dancing and promenade, with full bands of Music, from 9½ to 1, and 2½ to 6 o'clock. All these places were fully attended.

At the Music Hall, during the interval between the fourth and fifth performances on the programme of the first concert in the morning, His Honor Mayor Lincoln entered, escorting General Anderson and Admiral Farragut, who were greeted with loud cheers and tempestuous applause, waving of hats and handkerchiefs, every one rising in their seats.

The gentlemen being seated and the tumult subsiding, the Mayor came forward and said : —

My Friends : I thought to have the pleasure of introducing to you our noble guests here, but I perceive that they are already introduced and recognized by you, — bound to you heart to heart. Still, I will do myself the honor formally to present to you Vice-Admiral Farragut.

Admiral Farragut rose amid renewed and vociferous applause, and as soon as he could obtain silence, said : —

" It affords me great pleasure to return thanks to you for this greeting, and after an absence of forty years to meet you on this glorious day."

The Mayor : " And now for the hero of Fort Sumter :" (Great applause.)

General Anderson rose and said : —

" I can only thank you, as I do, from the bottom of my heart."

During the enthusiastic demonstrations of the audience which ensued, Miss Hattie Lincoln, daughter of His Honor the Mayor, presented to Admiral Farragut an elegant bouquet, and Miss Addie Standish, daughter of Alderman Standish, presented a similar one to General Anderson.

Mr. James R. Elliott than sang in fine style, " Columbia, the gem of the ocean," the audience joining in the chorus.

While singing the last verse, Mr. Elliott turned toward General Anderson and Admiral Farragut, singing these lines : —

> " May the wreaths they have worn never wither,
>   Nor the stars of their glory grow dim !
> May the service united ne'er sever,
>   But they to their colors prove true !
> Oh ! the Army and Navy forever !
>   Three cheers for the Red, White, and Blue ! "

Which were received with loud applause.   Alderman George W. Messinger then presented two very handsome bouquets to Misses Lincoln and Standish, and soon after His Honor the Mayor and his distinguished guests retired, and drove to Andrews Hall, where the General and Admiral were received with cheers from the children, who, at the Mayor's request, then sang a verse of "The Star-Spangled Banner." They thence proceeded to the Boston Theatre, the audience rising and the band in the balcony playing "Hail to the Chief," as they entered and advanced up the platform to the front of the stage, the young misses on the floor encircling the area in a double line.

Silence being restored, His Honor Mayor Lincoln said : —

" I beg to congratulate you all on the happy auspices of this occasion, and to present to you Vice-Admiral Farragut and Major-General Robert Anderson."

General Anderson thus replied to the loud applause of the youthful assembly : —

"My little friends, I wish that I could take you all by the hand and thank you for this welcome." (Great applause.)

Admiral Farragut said : —

" It affords me the deepest gratification to meet you on this glorious day, and to thank you for this complimentary reception." (Great applause and cheers.)

Nine young ladies in costume then came forward and danced the Highland Fling in a manner which was loudly applauded by the spectators. Mayor Lincoln and party withdrew shortly after, the band playing the National airs, and the large assembly cheering enthusiastically.

THE PROCESSION

was formed at City Hall (corner of Bedford and Chauncy streets) at ten o'clock. The Chief Marshal was Brevet Brig. Gen. Wm. S. Tilton, who was assisted by Col. P. R. Guiney,

Maj. J. Henry Sleeper, Capt. Nathan Appleton, and H. W. Tilton, Esq. as aids, and by the following assistant marshals: Lieut. Col. P. T. Hanley, Maj. J. W. Mahan, Capt. W. T. W. Ball, Capt. M. F. O'Hara, Capt. Wm. A. Hill, Lieut. C. F. Williams, Maj. W. T. Eustis, 3d, Maj. R. T. Lombard, Capt. Geo. D. Putnam, Capt. J. P. Jordan, Lieut. James Darling, Dr. E. G. Tucker, J. W. Wolcott, Jr., James H. Roberts, J. T. Fuller, Geo. F. Williams, Jr., Levi C. Barney, John D. Cadogan.

The procession marched in the following order : —

Twelve mounted Police Officers, in command of Sergeant John M. Dunn.

Col. Charles R. Codman and staff, in command of the escort.

Band from Gallop's Island.

Second Regiment of Infantry, under command of Lieut. Col. O. W. Peabody.

The Lincoln Guards of South Boston, Capt. M. E. Bigelow.

The Newton Zouaves, Capt. Alfred Schoff, a company of lads.

The 14th unattached Company of militia, Capt. Lewis Gaul.

Gilmore's Band with a Drum Corps.

The Boston Light Infantry Regiment, H. O. Whittemore, Captain commanding.

The 1st Battery Light Artillery, Capt. Cummings.

The 2d Battery Light Artillery, Capt. French.

Bond's Cornet Band.

Brig. Gen. Wm. S. Tilton, Chief Marshal, and Aids.

First Division. Col. Thomas Sherwin, Chief of Division. Aids, Capt. Geo. M. Barnard, Jr., and Lieut. John G. Kinsley.

This Division was composed of the City Government, various present and past City, County, and State officials, officers of the N. E. Veteran Association, invited guests, and the Boston Scottish Club in Highland costume, and the American Hibernian Society with their officers and beautiful banners in a carriage, the members following on foot in good numbers and wearing their handsome regalia.

Second Division. Col. A. F. Devereux, Chief of Division. Aids, Lieut. Col. W. S. Davis, and Capt. A. P. Martin. This Division was composed entirely of returned soldiers, headed by cavalrymen, preceded by a drum corps of young lads with Master Coflin, acting Drum Major.

Next was borne a banner on which was the motto, "The Nation's Defenders," who were represented by members of different Army Corps, each bearing a representation of their corps badge, as follows : —

1st Corps, " Buck's Eye."
2d Corps, " Clover."
3d Corps, " Diamond."
5th Corps, " Maltese Cross."
6th Corps, " Roman Cross."
9th Corps, " Anchor and Shield."
10th Corps, " Four-Bastioned Fort."
11th Corps, " Crescent."
20th Corps, " Heart."

Then came four large wagons, each drawn by four noble horses, furnished by Adams & Co.'s Express Company, and by

Jordan, Marsh, & Co., containing disabled veterans. As the brave and crippled men passed, the thousands of people who lined the sidewalks greeted them with hearty cheers.

The procession moved from City Hall in Chauncy Street, through Summer, Winter, Tremont, Park, and Beacon streets, to Arlington Street; through Arlington to Boylston Street; through Boylston to Park Square; through Park Square and Pleasant Street to Tremont Street; through Tremont, Dover, Washington, and Winter streets, to the Music Hall.

The City Council and guests entered Music Hall, and the escort conducted the veterans to the foot of Beacon Street Mall.

THE SOLDIERS' COLLATION.

Twenty tables were laid in Beacon Street Mall for the veteran returned soldiers and sailors, of which they partook with a hearty relish. After the eatables were disposed of, some of the veterans made brief remarks appropriate to the occasion, and among others Mr. Benjamin F. Norcross, a veteran sailor of thirty years' standing, who came home in the Canandaigua, made an interesting speech, which was listened to with marked attention. The company separated after giving cheers for the Army and Navy.

SERVICES IN THE MUSIC HALL.

The Music Hall was filled to overflowing. It had been appropriately draped, for the occasion, the names of the States and of John Hancock and the other signers of the Declaration of Independence, from Massachusetts, being prominent upon the galleries. There were also mottoes making proper allusion to the preservation of the Union by the valor of our brave men.

Soon after 12 o'clock, Mayor Lincoln entered with Admiral Farragut and Gen. Anderson, who were received with tremendous cheering. The singing of the " Star-Spangled Banner," which opened the exercises, was by a Choir selected from the High and Grammar schools, under the direction of Mr. Carl Zerrahn, and received much applause. A prayer was offered by Rev. Henry W. Foote, when the " Chorus of Pilgrims," from " I Lombardi," was sung.

The Declaration of Independence was gracefully read by Master Charles Harris Phelps. Rev. Mr. Manning, then delivered his Oration. It was warmly applauded, particularly the allusions to the suppressed passage of the Declaration of Independence, and to Farragut, Stringham, Grant, Sherman, Anderson, and President Lincoln, and the great act of his administration.

The following Original Hymn, by Mrs. Julia Ward Howe, was then sung to the Music of the " Old Hundredth Psalm."

> Our Fathers built the house of God;
>   Rough-hewn, with haste its slabs they laid;
> The savage man in ambush trod;
>   And still they worshipped undismayed.

> They wrought like stalwart men of war,
>   Who wrung the state from heathen hands;
> Who bore their faith's high banner far,
>   And in its name possessed the lands.

The skill of strife to peaceful arts,
  Their perils over, glad gave way;
The bond of freedom joined men's hearts
  More near than meaner compact may.

We, followers of their task and toil,
  Inherited their dangers too;
Drove bloody rapine from our soil,
  Th' oppressor dared, the murderer slew.

Our heavy work, like theirs, at end;
  Returning from the death-won field,
Brother with brother, friend with friend,
  Again the house of God we build.

Oh! may our ransomed freedom dwell
  In truth's own citadel secure;
And blameless guardians foster well
  The mystic flame that must endure.

The flame of holy human love,
  That makes our liberties divine;
Let each strong arm its champion prove,
  And each true heart its deathless shrine.

Benediction was pronounced by the Chaplain.

DINNER AT FANEUIL HALL.

At the close of the exercises at Music Hall, a procession
was formed of the City Council and its guests, which marched
directly to Faneuil Hall. The decorations of the Hall were
somewhat more carefully and elaborately arranged than is customary on such occasions, and are thus described by the
decorators, Messrs. Lamprell & Marble : —

"The entrance was through an arch of flags. From the centre of the ceiling was suspended a large star, twenty-five feet in diameter, composed of flags of all nations, in the centre of which was a blue field with silver stars. The points of the star were tipped with gilt ornaments. Radiating from the star were American pennants and various-colored bunting to the capital of each pillar; also red, white, and blue bunting extending around the cornice of the Hall. A large arch of green and gilt spanned the eagle, with a motto, "Peace — Reunion — Liberty." On the pillars were emblems of war, U. S. shield, liberty cap, &c. From the arch, and attached to the pillars, were a canopy of blue field, with stars, enveloping the eagle. On the panels of the Gallery were the names of some of our most prominent army and naval officers. On one side of the clock was "FARRAGUT — Welcome, in the Cradle of Liberty, to the noble leader of our brave and gallant Navy, who, in his own career, has embodied the loyalty, the valor, and the courage which has borne our hardy tars on to glorious victory." On the opposite side, "GRANT — All honor to the great Captain of the age, who combines the perseverance of Wellington with the strategy of Napoleon." On the side galleries, "MEADE," "SHERMAN," "SHERIDAN," "PORTER," "FOOTE," "STRINGHAM," "WINSLOW," and "ANDERSON" — Faithful among the faithless! Deserted by his Commander-in-Chief, he withstood all temptations, choosing death rather than the surrender of his country's flag to sedition and treason." Small glories of flags and shields were interspersed between the panels. White, red, and blue bunting extended in festoons around the base of the galleries, and

American flags and bunting were appropriately festooned in the rear of the rostrum. The lower windows were curtained with American flags and white, pink, and blue lace. The upper windows were decorated with flags of all nations. There were also large American flags on each side of the lower doors. Bronze medallions, life size, of the late President Lincoln, Secretary Seward, Lieutenant-General Grant, Major-General Meade, Major-General Butler, and Vice-Admiral Farragut, adorned the wall behind the Mayor's chair. On the rostrum in front, in the midst of a sea of beautiful mosses and flowers and aquatic plants, appeared a fine miniature representation of the U. S. ship Hartford, the flag-ship of Admiral Farragut at the battle of New Orleans."

His Honor Mayor Lincoln presided at the tables, and, upon his invitation, the Divine blessing was invoked by the Chaplain of the Day, Rev. Henry W. Foote.

The dinner was then spread, and the company occupied nearly an hour in the practical discussion of its merits. The cloth was then removed, when Mayor Lincoln rose and spoke as follows : —

" FELLOW-CITIZENS : Again, under happy auspices, we are assembled in Faneuil Hall, and, in company with distinguished guests, celebrate the anniversary of the Declaration of Independence. For the past four years our civic feast has been omitted. We have repaired to other temples, as has been the custom of the people of Boston on this day since the close of the Revolutionary War, and with prayer and praise have listened to those words of hope and cheer which were befitting the solemn exigency through which our country was passing; but our hearts were not attuned to those jubilant strains, which graced in happier times the festivities of our commemorative exercises.

"This venerated Hall, indeed, during this time, has not been closed. It has been exerting an influence from its traditional history, and from the live men whose eloquence has rung through its arches, as important as in any period since one stone was laid upon the other. Its doors have opened on their golden hinges to our armed men going to or coming from the gage of battle. They have been inspired by the patriotic memories which impregnate its walls. Their faith in the good old cause has been strengthened as they remembered the Fathers who rocked the cradle in the infancy of the Republic; and their indignation has been aroused as they heard the traitor's threat, that the Rebel flag would one day float over the sacred edifice. The stern discipline of sorrow and gloom was laid upon the land, to test the manhood of the people. The trial has been severe, and the sacrifice great; but through the Providence of God, and the might of the gallant men on the land and on the sea, who have unflinchingly stood by their country in its hour of peril, the Republic is saved, and we rejoice to-day with shouts of triumph unexampled in our history.

"What a contrast is the celebration of to-day to all which have preceded it! Before the late Rebellion, it was our custom to assemble to rehearse the noble story of our Fathers. Sometimes the thoughtful would raise the question if we of this generation were worthy of the rich inheritance they had bequeathed to us. We rejoiced, in holiday attire, over the deeds of our ancestors. Had a long peace and unexampled worldly prosperity sapped the foundations of public virtue? Had we become degenerate and unequal to the peculiar mission committed to us as one of the family of nations? The events of the last four years have answered these doubts. Our valor and mettle have been tried and tested; and we have shown to the world, and the record has been made on the historic page, that this people are 'worthy sons of worthy sires;' and that the impulses of a lofty patriotism beat as strongly in their bosoms as it did in the bosoms of those heroic men who pledged their lives and sacred honor, or stood the shock of battle in the war of the Revolution.

"The principles which they enunciated in the immortal document put forth to the world July Fourth, 1776, have received a more emphatic indorsement than even they were able to give them; and we stand to-day, in name and in spirit, in fact and in deed, a free and independent people. Chattel slavery, 'that thorn in the flesh,' which was so foreign to the genius of our Republican form of government, and which has had such an irritating influence upon the constitution of the body politic, no longer is a reproach to our fair name; and on this glorious anniversary, another race, born within the limits of the Republic, salutes our flag, as it rises in the morning's fresh light, as their emblem of freedom and manhood.

"We to-day commence a new epoch in the history of the nation. Assuming a position in the world which neither foreign nations nor domestic traitors can ever hereafter shake, our own military questions settled, we are to be called upon, as American citizens, to meet new duties and responsibilities growing out of an altered state of affairs. Following as a guide the principles laid down by the Fathers, instructed and enlightened by the events, recent and remote, which have transpired since the Federal Government was organized, crushing the spirit of despotism wherever it exists in old institutions, and infusing more of the spirit of liberty and humanity into all those which affect the present or the future happiness of the people, let patriotism, not party, be the touchstone to which every new measure of statesmanship shall be applied; and the world will be given to understand that the citizens of the United States are indeed, now and forever, ONE PEOPLE.

"Let a broad nationality which obliterates State lines be our absorbing passion. As our soldiers on the field, as our sailors on the deck, stood together in the late conflict with the Rebel foe, looking only to the one flag of the Union floating over them, so may we, bound together by the perils we have passed, become more firmly fixed in the resolve that the links which make these thirty-six commonwealths one nation shall never be severed.

"With these few observations, fellow-citizens, and congratulating you upon the inspiring circumstances under which we are celebrating the eighty-ninth anniversary of American Independence, with a cordial welcome to Faneuil Hall, to the brave men whose gallant exploits have given a new significance and glory to the hallowed observance of the day, cordially greeting at our festivities the heroic commander of Fort

10

Sumter, whose intrepid garrison first received and responded to the dastardly shots aimed at the honored ensign of the Republic, with a welcome as large as a sailor's heart to the Vice-Admiral, whose noble deeds have added to the fame as they have given a new name and rank to the navy of the United States, I will call upon you all, as loyal men, to rise while I propose the health of one who should be uppermost in our hearts to-day :—

"'His Excellency, Andrew Johnson, the President of the United States.'"

The Band played "The Star-Spangled Banner," the company standing.

The Mayor then introduced the Hon. John Lowell, Judge of the U. S. District Court, to respond to the sentiment just offered. Judge Lowell said : —

"I esteem myself peculiarly fortunate, Mr. Mayor, in being called upon to respond, at this precise time, to the loyal and ever-welcome sentiment — 'The President of the United States.'

"For the first time for four years we can hail the sentiment without misgiving and without drawback. No thought here and now of Presidents *de jure* and Presidents *de facto*: no subtle, unexpressed, irrepressible, afterthought, of 'so-called' Presidents, ruling over a 'so-called' nation within our own inherited domain. The 'so-called' are now busily engaged in throwing the blame upon each other, and ask of us only to be let alone, and need from us only Christian justice and Christian mercy. There is but one President now, thank God, from Canada to Mexico, and from the Atlantic to the Pacific seas.

" And the events of these four years of doubt, of struggle, and of progress, have taught us something about that great office itself, of which the brave, steady, thoroughly patriotic Andrew Johnson is now the worthy representative; have purged away, let us hope, some of the cankers of a full time and a long peace.

" In the course of that long period of prosperity, we had come to look upon the President of the United States too much as the mere chief of a successful party, as a gentleman who had a large number of party friends to reward, and of party enemies to punish, at the public expense; to the public damage, too often, for the men that he turned out of office (of whatever party) were, on the average, better than the men he put in, by an experience of four years in office. I appeal to every office-holder here if this will not be true — of his successor.

" We need to talk, jestingly, of loaves and fishes; but what were the five thousand and the seven thousand who were fed by these miracles to the swarms that infested Washington on the 4th of March of every fourth year? I guess all the white male citizens of Judea, with a considerable sprinkling of Assyrians thrown in (those Assyrians that ' came down ' to march farther than they intended), would hardly be a circumstance to the free and enlightened citizens of this Republic, who were ready to serve their country, in the interests of their party, in those happy days that are gone.

" But the war has taught us that the Presidents are intended for something besides making and unmaking tide waiters. Step by step, hour by hour, day by day, the man we had, by the blessing of an overruling Providence, chosen to do these little things, developed and grew to the height of ruling over many things, until on that fatal day in April there was scarcely a man in the civilized world that did not realize in Abraham Lincoln the fit constitutional chief of a great, persistent, magnanimous, and free people.

" He is gone! he is entered into the joy of his Lord. But his successor has, resting upon him, responsibilities scarcely less heavy, duties less conspicuous, but almost equally important. Let us give him — more than our respect — our love, our sympathy, and our prayers, that he may be enabled to conduct this nation wisely, humanely, safely through the shoals and breakers that still surround us, into the final haven of freedom, equality, and peace."

The Mayor next gave " The Commonwealth of Massachusetts." He remarked that no Executive of any Loyal State had been more zealous and efficient in upholding the Government in its efforts to restore the Union than His Excellency John A. Andrew, and he regretted that it was impossible for him to be present here. The Governor and the State were, however, well represented by Rev. S. K. Lothrop, D. D. who, as Chaplain of the Cadets, the Governor's body-guard, had been deputed by the Governor to appear in his place.

Dr. Lothrop spoke as follows : —

" Mr. Mayor and Fellow-Citizens : —

" I have had a great many pleasures and honors, sir, in my life, — more than I deserved, — but never such an honor as this, — that I should be called upon to respond for the Old

Commonwealth of Massachusetts, on the 4th of July, in Faneuil Hall, — an honor to which I have been summoned and detailed by his Excellency, the Governor, because I happened to be Chaplain to his Guard of Honor, the Independent Corps of Cadets, and I suppose that there is nobody between that humble office and his Excellency, who could be brought here to-day to speak for him.

"It is an honor which, in my most ambitious aspirings, I could never have dreamed would be mine, and therefore, Mr. Mayor and Fellow-Citizens, I beg you not to be surprised, should you perceive that the singular modesty for which I am known to be distinguished seems to be a little overborne by the extraordinary distinction which devolves upon me this day. If ever it was to devolve upon me to speak for the Commonwealth, I rejoice that it has come on an occasion of so much interest and importance as this year's Commemoration of our great National Anniversary ; and if I had to speak for any Governor, I am very glad to speak for Governor Andrew. He is a man of so much decision and independence of character, that doubtless there are many who do not entirely like him, but I may confidently assume that it will be admitted by the great mass of men in this State, of all parties, that he has presided over our State affairs with singular wisdom and energy during a period of great public peril and anxiety, and that through his unquestionable ability, through his untiring industry, through his political sagacity, through his undeviating and undaunted loyalty, he has so conducted his administration of our affairs for the last, now nearly, five years, as to make it form an interesting, important, brilliant, and glorious Chapter in the History of this Ancient

Commonwealth. I am not ' in the political line,' Mr. Mayor, but on the broad basis of a patriotic citizenship, I am ready to say, ' all honor to Governor Andrew, for the ability and fidelity with which he has upheld the honor of the State during these years of Civil War.' "

" But it is time, Mr. Mayor and gentlemen, that His Excellency should be permitted to speak for himself. With your leave, therefore, I will read a letter which he requested me to read on this occasion, which is as follows : —

" COMMONWEALTH OF MASSACHUSETTS, EXECUTIVE
" DEPARTMENT, BOSTON, June 30, 1865.

" HIS HONOR F. W. LINCOLN, JR., Mayor, Boston, Mass.

" MY DEAR SIR : My absence from Boston during a part of next week will prevent my enjoying the opportunity offered by your invitation to share with the City Government of Boston the festive commemoration of the anniversary of American Independence, which it is one of the distinctions of Boston that she always celebrates with a fervent and generous devotion, worthy the eminent fame of her ' Cradle of Liberty.'

" I think she is the only city in the Union of which it can be affirmed that this commemoration, in all the forms of the prophecy imputed to John Adams, is observed and kept by the municipality and by the people, in Peace and in War, without interruption, and with every emblem and demonstration of patriotic joy and gratitude.

" In 1859, I spent the 4th of July in the City of Washington, when, in conversation with a member of Mr. Buchanan's Cabinet, he remarked, with the twang and the peculiarity of emphasis which used to mark the conversation of the apostles and leaders of incipient treason : ' You Yankees are a singular people.' To which I gladly seized the occasion of replying : ' Indeed, we are, sir. In *Boston*, the metropolis of Yankeedom, this very Anniversary of American Liberty has been ushered in by a chorus of bells and of cannon. It is kept by our people as the " Sabbath day of Freedom." By processions, civic and military ; by solemn praise, and by a patriotic oration in the presence of the authorities and fathers of the city ; by a cheerful reunion of the representatives of the people and of every branch of the public service around the hospitable board where the Mayor in person presides ; by festivities and games for children of every class ; by sun-down guns and evening fireworks, attracting the whole population of Eastern Massachusetts,— by all these and by a universal holiday, these " singular Yankees" are remembering and celebrating this day. While here, at the seat of the Federal Government, I perceive only a few colored children of the Sunday schools marching in procession, alone and almost without human sympathy. I hope to see the day when something of our *singularity* may strike as high as the City of Washington.'

" He did not pursue the discussion. Since then I have thought, oh, how often ! of the poor little colored girls and boys, guarding as it were the few coals on that which should have been the *high altar*, and which have at last flamed up, with ample blaze, wafting to heaven the fragrant incense of a sublime devotion.

" Let these ' singular Yankees ' continue to be faithful to the ancient traditions. Let Boston assume and keep, if need be, in the lead of every true thought, of every noble purpose, and let the institutions and ideas which distinguish the people of New England be commended to every State and every section, until liberty shall be equally enjoyed by all the citizens of the Union in impartial participation.

" I have the honor to be, faithfully and respectfully, your friend and servant,

"JOHN A. ANDREW."

" It pleased His Excellency, Mr. Mayor and fellow-citizens, to ask me, after reading this letter, to make a few remarks of my own. But, sir, what can a man do who comes after the king, and what can I say that will add force or pertinence to the thoughts which I have just read? I am sure, fellow-citizens, our hearts must all sympathize with the spirit of this letter. The testimony which it bears to the extent and thoroughness, the constancy, the hearty and patriotic spirit with which the City of Boston at all times, in peace and in war, with every generation and without interruption, has celebrated the return of this Anniversary of American Independence, — that testimony is true, and for one I rejoice that Governor Andrew embraced the opportunity and had the courage to pour that testimony into the ears of the member of the Cabinet of Mr. Buchanan to whom he referred. Had he poured it into the ears and the heart of the Chief of that Cabinet, he would not have done any harm. (Applause.)

" It is to the glory of this city, — a glory which finds its reflection and its counterpart throughout Massachusetts and New England, — that, feeling the deep significance and importance of

the grand truths enunciated in the Declaration of Independence,
and reiterated in spirit in the preamble to the Constitution of
the United States, the people of Boston have always celebrated
the return of this day with various grateful demonstrations ; and
it is because they have thus celebrated it, that they can celebrate and have a right to celebrate it to-day with an unusual
display of patriotic pride and joy. Mr. Mayor, if there is a
man in this assembly whose heart does not beat with a deeper
throb of patriotic pride than ever before on the 4th of July, I
pity him. (Applause and ' Good.') But there is no such man
among you. I have done you injustice in supposing that it
could be so, because we celebrate this day this year under the
most grand and auspicious circumstances.

" We celebrate not simply our National Independence, but
our National deliverance and regeneration. We celebrate the termination of a four years' civil war unparalleled in the magnitude
of its operations, and in the transcendent importance of its
issues. (Applause.) We celebrate the extinction of that
which was the darkest blot upon our escutcheon ; we celebrate
the overthrow of a rebellion the most gigantic that ever threatened the life of a nation and failed of success,— a rebellion so
gigantic, so wide spread, so deep laid in its plans, so mighty in
its power and so determined in its purpose, that only a free
government and a free people could have triumphed over it.
(Long and continued applause.) I am reminded by the extinction of that rebellion, Mr. Mayor, and by all the desolation
it has spread in the States where it existed, of some strong and
striking words uttered more than thirty years ago by Edward
Everett, whose spirit is with us this day, whose image is in all

11

our hearts. Oh, would that he was present with his magic voice
to utter the words of eloquence and power which this occasion
would call from his lips! In 1833 he delivered the 4th of July
oration at Worcester. It was just after General Jackson, sup-
ported by the irresistible logic, the broad statesmanship, and the
mighty power of Daniel Webster, had put down nullification in
South Carolina (Applause), 'scotched the serpent but not killed
it.' Mr. Everett's oration, therefore, was largely occupied with
the value and importance of Union; and therefore he said:
'I would not have it supposed that I think the Union is of
special value and importance to the people of this section of the
country. The intimation which has been thrown out, the belief
which has been in some quarters avowed that the Northern
States have a peculiar interest in the preservation of the Union,
— that they derive advantages from it at the uncompensated
expense of the South, — is the greatest delusion that was ever
propagated by men deceived themselves, or disposed to deceive
others. All parts of the Union would suffer deplorably from
the dissolution of it, but the bitter chalice would not be presented first to our lips. The people of the North would suffer
from the dissolution of the Union, but they would be the last to
suffer and they would suffer least, while that portion of the
country that is continually shaking over us the menace of dissolution would be swept with the besom of destruction the moment
an offended Providence permitted that ill-starred purpose to
reach to maturity.' (Applause.) Sir, these words, which I
quote from memory, but I believe quite correctly, uttered more
than thirty years ago by the scholar, the statesman, the orator
who did so much by his moderation and forbearance to prevent

the late rupture, and who, when that rupture came, stood firm in a manly loyalty, and did good and noble service for the Union, — these words now come up before us as a prophecy awfully fulfilled. The desolate plantations, the ruined towns and villages, the multitude of battle fields, the whole scene throughout that whole region of country from the Potomac to the Mississippi, bears testimony that the bitter chalice has not been held to our lips, but to the lips of those who undertook to overthrow our Government.

"Mr. Mayor, our country began with God. Our fathers planted the first germs of our civilization in a spirit of Christian faith, amid sacrifices and tears, and from that hour, all through our history, the providence of God has been marvellously displayed in our growth, preservation, and national development, and more marvellously than all in the way in which that providence has led us on, and led us through this great struggle with a glorious triumph of liberty, a better, larger, and more established freedom. And this day and every day, our thought should first mount up in gratitude and adoration to the God of our fathers for all that goodness to them and to us and to our country under which we meet together here to-day. (Applause.) And next to God and under his Providence, our thoughts should go forth in honor, in admiration, in reverence and in gratitude to the noble defenders of our country and its liberties (loud applause), to all those of every rank, high and low, who took their lives in their hands and went forth to fight for the dear old flag, 'The Stars and the Stripes;' and who have so fought for it, that now with a fresh glory around it, with the power of a free people still slumbering in its folds, it floats undisturbed over the land, waves its protection and its power alike over an unbroken Union, an undivided country. (Loud applause.) And I rejoice, sir, I sympathize with you and with all my fellow-citizens, that it is permitted us this day to behold the faces of two of these noble and gallant defenders. (Tremendous applause.)

" I thank God that I have an opportunity to look into the face and to cry honor to the man who in those gloomy days in the Spring of 1861 stood there at Fort Sumter alone, as it were, unaided, unreached, undirected even by his Government, stood there firm and resolute in the difficult duty of forbearance and inaction so long as they were his duty,— brave and resolute in resistance when the hour for resistance came, and continued that resistance so long as seventy half-starved men could fight against ten thousand. (Tremendous applause and three cheers for General Anderson.)

"And I thank God, sir, that it is permitted me and my fellow-citizens to look upon the face, to welcome to our hearts and our homes, to our city and to this old Cradle of Liberty, and to cry honor to the man who has written a new and brilliant chapter in the history of naval warfare (tremendous applause),— a chapter fit to succeed those that tell of the exploits of Perry and McDonough, of Hull and Morris, of Preble and Decatur, and many others that I might mention, and who has so written that new and brilliant chapter in naval history, that when it comes to be thoroughly read and understood, the halo of glory that gilds the names of Nelson and Trafalgar will grow pale before the grander glory that shall gather, in every American heart, around the names of Farragut and Mobile. (Thundering cheers, the company all rising.)

" Mr. Mayor, I have spoken much too long. I will stop. I will crush down a great many thoughts that swell in my heart for utterance,— thoughts connected with our martyred President and his noble character,— thoughts connected with the memory of our noble dead of this State and of every State, the pride and flower of the nation,— thoughts connected with the difficulties and the glories that encompass this nation in its present condition and prospects, with the great moral and physical power it is to become in the world if true to itself, its opportunities, and its principles. I feel much and deeply upon all these topics, Mr. Mayor, and I should like to talk about them, but I will crush them all down and say, in conclusion, that while I honor the Union, while I cleave to it and will cling to it to the death, while I am ready to maintain it at all hazards and at every cost, I honor Old Massachusetts as a glorious part of this Union. (Applause.)

" I honor it for what it has done for itself. I honor it for what it has done for the Union, — for all the thoughts, influences, and actions which it has sent out into the Union, and I am ready to conclude and to agree with the Governor in saying, let these singular Yankees continue faithful to the traditions. Let Boston assume, and if need be take the lead in every true thought and in every right purpose ; and let the institutions and the ideas which distinguish the people of New England be commended to every State and every section until liberty is universally enjoyed by every citizen of the Union in impartial participation. The ideas and institutions of New England are only two,— a common school in every hamlet, and a church in every village. (Applause.) Let these institutions go forth, let there be intellectual and moral culture everywhere for all, and then the wider our freedom, the greater our glory, the more secure our safety." (Loud applause.)

At the close of Dr. Lothrop's remarks, His Honor the Mayor stated that an emblem of peace lay concealed among the flowers upon the table, and releasing a dove from its confinement, the bird made a circling flight, and perched upon the gilded eagle surmounting the picture of the Webster and Hayne debate. The episode excited hearty applause.

The next sentiment given was, — " The Memory of Abraham Lincoln," which was received by the company standing and in silence, the band playing a dirge.

The Mayor then introduced to the company, Brevet Major General Robert Anderson, with a few complimentary remarks. He alluded to the fact that, notwithstanding the pressure brought to bear upon him, in consequence of his Southern birth, to desert his flag, he remained steadfast to the Union, and by his heroic defence of Sumter, though apparently defeated, really united and fixed the loyal sentiment of the country.

Gen. Anderson was received with a round of cheers, and spoke as follows : —

" My FRIENDS : You must not expect a speech from me. Retired from the army, after a consultation with a board of physicians, on a declaration of my doctors that my brain had been over-taxed, and that I would never be fit again for duty, I have, since that time, been prohibited from attempting to make a speech.

"I am indebted to Massachusetts for many things; and, before I sit down, I will simply remark that the first letter I received in Fort Moultrie, before I went to Fort Sumter, when it was found that things were looking very threatening, — (I felt the storm there long before you saw the flash here), — I received a letter from a gentleman (I am sorry I don't remember his name), a militia officer of this city, offering me troops from Massachusetts if the Government would then allow them to be sent to me.* (Applause.)

"Gentlemen, after what I have said, you will excuse me from attempting to make any further remarks. I thank you from the bottom of my heart for the kind reception you have given me in this noble, this great Hall, on this grand occasion. We have a country again, and, thank God! we have a country of which we can all be proud. (Applause.)

"Our country has passed through a storm such as no other country ever passed through or was threatened with before. Let us give to God thanks for the victory which our troops by His blessing have been enabled to win for us." (Applause.)

The Mayor then presented to the company Vice-Admiral David G. Farragut, remarking that the City was extremely fortunate in having for its guest such eminent representatives of the Army and Navy. The great events in the brilliant career of Admiral Farragut were already as familiar and dear to American hearts as "household words."

---

* At the reception given by Gen. Anderson and Admiral Farragut, to the citizens of Boston, in Faneuil Hall, on the next day (July 5) Brig. Gen. Edward W. Hinks was introduced to Gen. Anderson as the officer who sent the letter alluded to.

The Admiral was received most enthusiastically, and after the restoration of silence, spoke as follows : —

"Mr. Mayor and Gentlemen : In the first place I don't really know what I could say. These gentlemen have already gone over the ground. The first speaker gave us a synopsis of the war ; the next eulogized it, and I really feel that I have nothing left but to talk about myself which would be a most unprofitable thing both to you and me. ("Go on.") It has simply been my good fortune to be associated with many Massachusetts troops during the war, and it gives me great pleasure to testify to their good conduct ; and it has always given me great pleasure and satisfaction in every instance where we have worked together, that we have always worked in harmony and in good faith with one another. I am extremely obliged to you for this reception, and it is a most happy circumstance that I, — after having left this port nearly fifty years ago, as the Mayor said (I was then a little midshipman),— should return here as Vice-Admiral on this great and grand occasion, the 4th of July, after a peace which I predicted a year ago last June would soon come, — and should be greeted by you for that which you conceive to have been my great exertions during the war to bring about that peace." (Applause.)

The Mayor then proposed, — "The Orator of the day. He has said the right thing, in the right way, and in the right place."

Rev. Mr. Manning expressed his thanks for the honor conferred upon him, and for the complimentary sentiment given by the Mayor, but excused himself from making any remarks.

In the absence of Col. Wm. S. King, who was expected to respond to "The Citizen Soldiery of Massachusetts," Mayor Lincoln called upon Col. P. R. Guiney, late of the Ninth Mass. Volunteers.

Col. Guiney said that "he regretted Col. King's absence, as he considered him a true and eloquent representative of the Citizen Soldiers, but there was some compensation in the fact that we had with us the great Admiral, who might be called the *King* of the seas. These are the only sort of Kings that will take root on this continent.

"For two reasons it is unnecessary to say much about the citizen soldiers of Massachusetts. They are content that the honors and enthusiasm of this occasion should be absorbed by the two illustrious heroes whose presence gives such charm and force to our festivities, and who are so deeply loved by every soldier of our State. Then it is not necessary to say much about Massachusetts soldiers. Words used in their praise, unless very carefully selected, would be apt to detract from, rather than to enhance the idea of their real merit. Indeed, every battle-field of our country, as well as the slaughter prison-houses of the South, — wherever endurance, heroism, and devotion to the Republic were required, — gave testimony that the deeds of our citizen soldiery, baffled and conquered two things, rhetoric and the enemy. The latter has not recovered yet.

"To be brief, then : in war, the citizen soldiers of Massachusetts are the unrelenting foes of all who assail our flag or our liberties ; in peace, in politics, they are inclined to think that liberty has been long enough regulated and proscribed by law, and that it is now time to recognize it as a first principle, that law should be regulated by that liberty which was anterior to it, and which it never could rightfully crush or impair."

The Mayor then gave, — "The loyal women of America," which was responded to by Mr. Charles W. Slack, who said : —

"Mr. Mayor and Gentlemen : It is most fitting that these festive exercises should not close without an appreciative word for the women of America.

"'The loyal women of America !' — how sweetly floats in that phrase, with the glad rejoicings of this national birthday, the crowding remembrances of this more than hallowed anniversary ! Amid the salvos of artillery, the pealing of bells, the gayly waving colors, the honors to brave men, mingling in the festivities of this Ancient Hall, and lending transcendent merit to the public rejoicings of this day the continent over, come precious thoughts of the labors and prayers of the loyal, queenly women of America, through all the struggles and anxieties of the great contest now happily passed. They deserve our heartiest, truest thanks. From the full well of individual and national gratitude must they ever be permitted to draw unstinted draughts.

"From every rank, class, and condition, — the poor girl picking berries by the roadside, that, converted into money, might help; the aged matron, late into the night, finishing off the comforting sock for the distant volunteer; the wealthy lady of the city giving her thirtieth, or more, monthly contribution, — ay ! from the humble black slavewoman of the South, whose heart welcomed and whose cake nourished our exhausted boys flying from the charnel-houses of Rebel detention, to those magnificent parliaments of accomplished womanhood all over the land that inaugurated soldiers' fairs, and sailors' homes, — how cheerfully, how nobly came the requisite help, — the patient, confident, untiring labor, — that now throws such a halo around the nation's triumphs by land and sea!

"We cannot forget the women of America if we would! When the brilliant record of this war shall be fully made up, with the deeds of heroic men, the skill of counsellors, and the steadfast devotion of the citizen, will be mentioned in glowing page and sympathetic verse those quieter and gentler, it may be, but no less valuable and welcome, labors of the loyal women of our land. Indeed, that the oldtime nationality of our flag, the maintenance of our institutions, and the perpetuity of the Republic, are as much owing to the unwearied efforts and influence of the women, in camp, hospital, and at home, as to heroism on the field or shipboard, is a belief that many entertain, and which has often been expressed. Accepting this thought, may we now, in the twilight hour of this festal day, with the music of bells and cannon in parting salute honoring this doubly endeared anniversary, pass from this Hall with sincere ascription to God in heart and upon lip, as we remember with gratitude and joy the services of 'The loyal women of America!'"

His Honor then proposed as the final sentiment, "The Declaration of Independence," to which Mr. Charles Harris Phelps eloquently responded as follows: —

"Mr. Mayor and Gentlemen: It would be improper and out of place in me, indebted as I am to my position for the privilege of being called upon, to presume to eulogize or to praise the Declaration of Independence. No words of mine can add to its fame or increase its renown. But as I stood in the Music Hall, and read the inscription, 'Our brave men have preserved our Union,' I could not but feel how weakly and with how little meaning its glowing words were being read, compared to the significance which Anderson gave it as he read it to Rebeldom by the thunders of Sumter's cannon, — compared to the meaning which Farragut gave it by his double-shotted broadsides in the harbor of Mobile (applause), — to the meaning given it by a million of bayonets under Grant and Sherman and Sheridan, as they read it on every battle-field of the South with the emphasis of resounding arms and salvos of artillery. (Loud applause.)

"These heroes, illustrious through all time, whose fame shall be sounded in every tongue, have, during the past four years, declared that 'all men are created equal,' in such a manner that all traitors have trembled and all nations rejoiced. But it is not for me to trespass further upon your patience, neither is the occasion nor the theme from my humble lips, and I only ask your permission to offer a toast to

" 'Our gallant Army and Navy — The best readers of the Declaration of Independence, they have sent it in thunder-tones to all the world. Let the oppressed of every nation hear and take courage.' "

The benediction was then pronounced by Rev. Mr. Manning.

THE REGATTA

was appointed to take place on Charles River in the morning at 8 o'clock, that being the hour of high tide. An immense assemblage was present, and from the numerous entries, it was expected that the races would be unusually interesting and exciting. Unfortunately, however, the wind rose before the conclusion of the first race so as to make it dangerous for the light shell-boats to attempt to go over the course, and it was found necessary to put off the race to a later hour in the day, the people being notified, as far as practicable, of the postponement.

The first race was for single scull oarsmen, there being seven entries. The principal contest, however, was between James Hammill, of Pittsburg, Pa., champion oarsman of America, and John H. Radford of New York, who has won several races; and although the latter obtained a considerable lead at the start, he was soon passed by Hammill, who won easily. The others, finding it useless to contend, drew out before completing the first mile.

The next race was for four-oared boats, the prizes offered being larger than usual; and though there were four boats entered, but two appeared to contend. These were the famous "Geo. L. Brown Crew," of New York, so often successful in these waters, and the "Geo. B. McClellan Crew," of Boston and St. John. The distance being six miles, an opportunity was afforded the spectators to see a turn at the lower stake, but as the "Brown" crew, in their new boat, the "Samuel Collyer," were well ahead and appeared to be winning easily, the excitement was not wrought to a very high pitch.

The third race was for double sculls, and was won easily by John Hammill and William Jackson, of Pittsburg, a boat rowed by McKee and Daily, of Boston being second. A boat from Harvard College, the "Winona," was well up with the winner at the stake, but the wind having freshened, they shipped a good deal of water and were compelled to abandon the struggle.

The evening was now pretty well advanced, and there remained on the programme a race for six-oared boats, for which were entered the "P. L. Tucker," of New York (rowed by the "Brown Crew"), and two Harvard College boats. The weather had, however, become so unpropitious, that the Harvard boys did not feel safe to row. So there could be no race. Efforts were made to induce the boats to row the next day, but the New York party were anxious to return home, and the matter was dropped.

The following is a summary of the races : —

First Race, for single sculls and wherries : distance two miles.

James Hammill, of Pittsburg.   Time, 16 min. 28½ sec. First Prize, $ 100.

John H. Radford, of New York.   Time, 16 min. 38 sec. Second Prize, $ 50.

T. M. Doyle, of Boston.   Time not taken.

Jere Driscoll, of Boston.   Time not taken.

Second Race : for four-oared boats : distance six miles.

" Samuel Collyer," rowed by James H. Biglin, John A. Biglin, Bernard Biglin, and D. Leary, of New York. Time 43 min. 32 sec. First Prize $ 400.

" George B. McClellan," rowed by John Morris, of St. Johns, and George Faulkner, John Lambert, and Thomas Scott, of Boston. Time, 43 min. 47 sec. According to the Rules no Second Prize was awarded.

Third Race : for double scull boats : distance two miles.

" Sam Collins," rowed by John Hammill, and William Jackson, of Pittsburg. Time, 17 min. 54 sec. First Prize $ 100.

" Voyageur," rowed by A. McKee, and J. Daily of Boston. Time, 18 min. 4 sec. Second Prize $ 50.

" Winona," rowed by C. E. Hubbard and S. R. Holdredge, of Cambridge.

" J. Hancon," rowed by J. Driscoll and J. Donahue, of Boston.

Fourth Race : for six-oared boats : distance three miles.

" P. L. Tucker," entered by the Biglin Brothers, Leary, Eckerson, and Burns, of New York.

" Harvard," entered by the University Crew of Cambridge.

" 68," entered by the Freshman Class of Harvard College.

This race could not take place on account of the rough water.

THE BALLOON ASCENSIONS.

Owing to the strong westerly wind which prevailed, Prof. King considered it inexpedient as well as unsafe to inflate either of his balloons and attempt ascensions, either alone or with companions. Consequently no ascension was made from the Common, greatly to the disappointment of the thousands present. On the Saturday following the two balloons were sent up successfully, and made very pleasant voyages ; one to Melrose, and the other to Scituate.

THE FIREWORKS.

The display of fireworks in the evening, was furnished by C. E. Masten, of Roxbury. Some of the principal pieces were very good. The piece constituting the grand finale was partially destroyed, the framework having been blown over by a sudden squall of wind in the early part of the evening. The line pieces, however, with that portion where a salvo of artillery is heard, and two gunboats, one upon either hand, bearing the names of " Farragut " and " Porter," move from left to right, the batteries firing a national salute, was preserved and made a fine closing display. The fireworks at East and South Boston passed off successfully.

CORRESPONDENCE.

CORRESPONDENCE.

The following were among the responses received to the invitations to participate in the Celebration : —

TREASURY DEPARTMENT, *June* 15, 1865.

DEAR SIR : Your favor of the 8th inst. is received. I spent some of my early and happiest days in Boston ; I feel that I have a right, therefore, almost to claim to be one of her citizens ; and am proud that she has not only maintained her Revolutionary reputation, but added largely to it by her devotion to the country in the great conflict now brought to a glorious termination by the utter overthrow of the Rebellion, which, for the past four years, has been threatening the existence of the Union.

I am gratified to learn that it is the intention of her citizens to celebrate the approaching Fourth of July with unusual ceremony. Nothing but imperative official engagements will prevent me from accepting your kind invitation to be present with you on this interesting occasion.

Please accept my thanks for the honor you have done me, and believe me to be,

Very truly yours,

HUGH McCULLOCH.

Hon. F. W. Lincoln, Jr. *Mayor of Boston, Mass.*

WASHINGTON, *July* 1, 1865.

Dear Sir: I am honored by your invitation to partake of the hospitality of the City of Boston, and unite with you in celebrating the approaching Anniversary of the Declaration of Independence.

It is gratifying to witness the arrangements which are being made throughout the country the present year for the general observance of this anniversary, which, during our civil troubles has been, to some extent, neglected. May we not hope that the successful termination of the war for the Union will destroy that sectional animosity which prevailed for a period, and restore harmony and good will among our countrymen? The disturbing element in our national affairs having been removed, there is now no cause or pretext for alienation. Hereafter the States will act on terms of more perfect equality, and as long as each shall discharge its appropriate duties and respect the right of others, each and all of them sustaining in good faith the Federal Government in the exercise of its authority, no serious dissension can exist, and our national unity will be preserved and strengthened.

Under the benignant auspices of peace and union, the approaching National Anniversary should be universally commemorated.

Boston, with her Revolutionary history, her patriotic traditions, and her intelligent loyalty, will, I doubt not, observe the day in a manner worthy of her ancient renown. My engagements are such, however, that I shall be compelled to deny myself the pleasure of partaking of the hospitality to which you have invited me, and of uniting with you in your celebration. I have the honor to be,

Very respectfully,

GIDEON WELLES.

Hon. F. W. Lincoln, Jr. *Mayor of Boston.*

———

Boston, *July* 1, 1865.

My dear Sir: It will not be in my power to unite with my fellow-citizens of Boston in celebrating the Anniversary of our National Independence; but I rejoice that we can celebrate so happily, with Victory as the mistress of ceremonies.

Do not, I pray you, Mr. Mayor, let the great day pass without reminding our fellow-citizens that victory on the field of battle is not enough. There must be that further victory which will be found in the recognition everywhere in the country of the ideas of the Declaration of Independence. All must confess that, according to these ideas, there can be no republican government, which is not founded on " the consent of the governed" and the equality of all persons before the law. And all must dedicate themselves to the work of establishing these ideas.

Then will our Fathers be vindicated and our country be glorified. God save the Republic!

Accept my thanks for the invitation with which you have honored me.   And believe me, dear sir,

Faithfully yours,

CHARLES SUMNER.

The Mayor of Boston.

To His Honor, Frederic W. Lincoln, Jr. *Mayor of the City of Boston :* —

Dear Sir : I beg leave to express, through you, to the Committee on Invitations of the City Council of Boston, my very grateful acknowledgments for the honor of their invitation to unite with them in the celebration of the approaching Anniversary of American Independence.   The public observance of the day, by the municipal authorities, and my more immediate fellow-citizens, *of this city*, seems to dictate the greater propriety of my remaining here ; but, whether here or there, my sentiments and sympathies will be with the joyous commemoration of the occasion.   Every loyal heart must alike swell with gratitude, in recognition of the glorious triumphs of the past, and in the better hopes, assurances, and safeguards, which peace now brings to a sustained Government, a restored Union, and a gallant, patriotic, and free people.

I have the honor to be, sir, with the most respectful regard,

Your obliged and obedient servant,

LEVI LINCOLN.

Worcester, *June* 30, 1865.

NEW YORK, *June* 14, 1865.

Hon. F. W. Lincoln, Jr. *Mayor of Boston :—*

Dear Sir : I have just received your letter of yesterday, inviting me to be present at the proposed observance, by your City, of the approaching Anniversary of the Declaration of Independence.

The occasion, the place, and the time, all concur to make me deeply regret that engagements here render the acceptance of your kind invitation impossible. I can only express my cordial sympathy with your determination to give the ceremonies " a more imposing character than usual." It is right that the country, which has just put down, by courage and self-sacrifice, the most gigantic treason the world has ever witnessed, should make a demonstration of its thankfulness, which shall correspond with the magnitude of the perils it has escaped ; and it is eminently appropriate that among the foremost to give utterance to the sentiments the surrounding circumstances are calculated to inspire should be your city, which was among the most efficient in establishing our Independence, and which has labored with such patriotic zeal and unswerving resolution to maintain the Union of the States.

Very truly yours,

JOHN A. DIX.

———

HEAD-QUARTERS ARMY OF THE POTOMAC, *June* 22, 1865.

To the Hon. F. W. Lincoln, Jr. *Mayor of Boston, Mass.*

Dear Sir : I have the honor to acknowledge the receipt of your polite letter of the 18th inst., inviting me to Boston on the approaching Anniversary of the Declaration of Independence; and to express my great regret, that, owing to a prior engagement to visit Gettysburg, it will not be in my power to accept your invitation. It would afford me much pleasure to visit Boston, a city so distinguished during this great war for its patriotism, illustrated by the valor of so many of its citizens on fields where I have had the honor to command, and I trust I shall have this gratification before the summer has passed.

In the mean time, I beg you will accept my thanks for the compliment you have honored me with, and believe me to be, with sincere respect,

Your most obedient servant,

GEO. G. MEADE,

Maj. Gen. U. S. A.

War Department, Adjutant-General's Office,

Washington, *June* 26, 1865.

His Honor F. W. Lincoln, Jr. *Mayor of Boston, and others of Committee on Invitations.*

Gentlemen : I have had the honor to receive your invitation to unite with the City Council of Boston in celebrating the approaching Anniversary of the Declaration of American Independence.

I regret that reasons of a public character will prevent my being absent at this time from Washington, but assure you that nothing could more gratify me than to be present in my native city on this most interesting occasion, when it would seem an unusual significance will attach to our National Anniversary, when we may on that day proclaim to the world that our form of Government is no longer an " Experiment," but a thing thoroughly tried and established.

With great respect and esteem, I have the honor to be, Gentlemen,

Your obedient servant,

E. D. TOWNSEND,

Asst. Adj. Gen. U. S. A.

WASHINGTON, *June* 29, 1865.

To THE MAYOR AND CITY COUNCIL OF BOSTON : —

GENTLEMEN : I duly appreciate the honor of your invitation to unite with you in celebrating the approaching Anniversary of the Declaration of American Independence, and regret that previous engagements will probably deprive me of that great pleasure.

It is the first occasion of the kind on which the country stands before the world, having made good the first pledge of our Constitution. We are indeed a Nation of Freemen.

To that end we have not spared treasure, nor lives far beyond price.

One great question remains, but that will be worked out in the appointed time by the wisdom of our people, so that justice shall be done to all.

In these results your noble city has borne her full part. It was a regiment of your citizens that made its way to the Capital in that anxious hour when only a handful of men, of which I was one, had gathered about the Government of the Union. The massive array of that legion, as it moved along the avenue gave an assurance that cheered every heart.

On another occasion I was present when the 54th rushed upon the parapets of Wagner. Many brave men laid down life there, but none more lamented than the gallant Colonel Shaw.

For every day of the last four years I have given my most earnest efforts to the great cause. One of my sons can say as much, and among other results participated at Vicksburg and Fort Fisher. Another only ceased when life was spent, in an attempt to free our captive soldiers from the dungeons of Richmond. So that all of my name that could bear arms, were at their posts.

With my best wishes for the prosperity of the City of Boston, I have the honor to be,

Your obedient servant,

J. A. DAHLGREN,

Rear-Admiral U. S. Navy.

NEW YORK, *June* 29, 1865.

GENTLEMEN: Your circular of invitation, enclosing a ticket to the City of Boston 89th Anniversary Celebration of the American Independence, was duly received.

To participate in such a celebration in the old Cradle of Liberty, at such a time, would afford me an extraordinary pleasure; of which I shall be deprived by the inexorable commands of duty. But I join with you, and all true friends of freedom and justice, in heartfelt thanks to the all-bounteous Giver of all good, for having brought this nation out of its late peril, and in imploring Him " who maketh to be of one mind the people of a city," to keep this great Republic one and indivisible now and forever.

Yours truly,

W. S. ROSECRANS, *Major-General.*

To F. W. LINCOLN, JR. MAYOR, *and others of Committee, Boston, Mass.*

ENGINEER'S OFFICE, DEFENCES OF BOSTON HARBOR,
July 1, 1865.

HON. F. W. LINCOLN, JR. *Mayor of Boston:* —

SIR: I have the honor to acknowledge the receipt last evening of the invitation of the authorities of this city to be present at their celebration of the coming 4th of July. And though a previous acceptance of another invitation to be present at an adjoining State celebration, prevents my having the pleasure of accepting yours, I cannot refrain from the expression of my congratulations to this principal city of that State, which, with the governor, has done so much to make this day of all others so worthy of a grand celebration. For this is the first 4th of July in all our history that has really found us a free people ; for, though the chains of Great Britain have long ago been thrown off, as they were *nominally,* upon the first of these great days, it is but now that the shackle of the slave has fallen, and the political tyranny over the North has ceased, leaving us for the first time as a people " born free and equal." God grant that such justice shall be meted out to the wrong-doers that we shall never be in their thraldom again.

Very respectfully your obedient servant,

H. W. BENHAM, *Brevet Major-General.*

PHILADELPHIA, PA., *June* 27, 1865.

DEAR SIR: I have the honor to acknowledge the receipt of your invitation to become the guest of the City of Boston on the approaching 4th of July.

Please accept my thanks for the compliment, and my regret that I cannot be present, owing to a previous engagement from the Committee in charge of the celebration at Gettysburg. As several officers who served under my command in that battle desire to revisit the field in my company, I do not feel at liberty to disregard the arrangement already made.

The defence of the flag of the Union in Charleston Harbor, at the commencement of the Rebellion, drew its inspiration from the opening scenes of the Revolution in the vicinity of Boston. I am glad to learn that Gen. Anderson has promised to be with you, for I think it peculiarly appropriate that Fort Sumter should do honor to Bunker Hill.

I am sir,

Your obedient servant,

A. DOUBLEDAY,
Major-General Volunteers.

To HIS HONOR, MAYOR LINCOLN, *of Boston, Mass.*

www.ingramcontent.com/pod-product-compliance
Lightning Source LLC
Chambersburg PA
CBHW032148010726
47493CB00008BA/2637